DISNEY's
PIRATES of the CARIBBEAN

Book of the Films

This is a Parragon book
First published in 2006

Parragon
Queen Street House
4 Queen Street
Bath, BA1 1HE, UK

ISBN 1-40548-318-0
Printed in Italy

DISNEY'S

PIRATES of the CARIBBEAN

THE CURSE OF THE BLACK PEARL

Adapted by Irene Trimble
Still photography by
Elliott Marks and John Bramley

Based on the screenplay
by Ted Elliott and Terry Rossio
and Jay Wolpert
Produced by Jerry Bruckheimer
Directed by Gore Verbinski

Chapter
1

Listen here: long ago, there was a legend of a ghostly black ship that sometimes appeared when the fog grew thick. Aye, its sails were big and black – as though they had been cut from shadow and sewn with sin. The timbers had been stained dark with the blood of innocent souls unlucky enough to cross the black ship's path. And its crew, it was said, were pirates all, cursed to sail forever under a foul wind of murder and mischief.

But of course, a tale like that would be nothin' but a sailor's old ghost story. And you don't believe in ghosts . . . do you?

The fog was dreadful. Still, the pride of the Royal Navy, the HMS *Dauntless*, kept its course.

Armed with 50 guns and a crew tough enough to make any pirate take pause, the *Dauntless* swept slowly onwards through the dark sea.

Standing alone at the ship's bow was its youngest passenger. Elizabeth Swann was her name. Her small hands clutched the rail as she shivered in the cold. Elizabeth was not a bit afraid of what might lie in wait in the fog. She secretly thought it would be exciting to meet a real pirate. She remembered a song from long ago, and slowly, into the grey mist, she began to sing:

"Yo ho, yo ho, a pirate's life for me,
Yo ho, yo ho, a pirate's life–"

Suddenly, a hand reached out and clutched her shoulder. "Quiet, missy!" snarled a seaman. "Cursed pirates sail these waters! You want to call 'em down on us?"

Elizabeth, then only 12 years old, stared wide eyed into the weather-beaten face.

"Mr Gibbs!" Captain Norrington snapped at the old sailor.

"But she was singin' about pirates," Gibbs

protested. "Bad luck to sing about pirates with us mired in this unnatural fog . . . mark my words."

Elizabeth knew that she was expected to behave. She was on her way to Port Royal, Jamaica, where her father was going to be governor. "We must comport ourselves as befits our class," he reminded her as he joined her on deck. Elizabeth nodded, but in her heart, she still wished to meet a pirate one day.

Quietly, she looked back out over the rail and stared into the deep green water. Suddenly, she noticed something afloat on the waves. It was a parasol – a sight that much delighted Elizabeth. She was wondering where it could have come from when a much larger shape slowly floated out on the foam. "Look!" she shouted, pointing over the side. A still body was now drifting towards the ship.

Captain Norrington reacted quickly. "Man overboard!" he shouted.

But Elizabeth could see that it wasn't a man. "Boy overboard!" she added, recognizing the person in the water to be someone about her own age.

"Fetch a boat hook and haul him out of there!" Captain Norrington ordered the men on deck. Elizabeth watched the crew of the *Dauntless* swing the boat hooks and snag the limp body as it passed the ship.

Governor Swann helped Captain Norrington drag the boy aboard as Elizabeth moved in for a closer look.

"He's still breathing!" declared Norrington, his ear down by the boy's mouth.

"But where did he come from?" asked Governor Swann.

The men of the *Dauntless* stood silent. The eyes of every crewman were searching the sea for an answer when Gibbs suddenly gasped. "Mary, mother of God!"

Looking out on the water, Elizabeth could now see the wreckage of a ship, along with the bodies of its crew. Then, slowly emerging from the fog, came the charred and burning hull of the doomed ship itself.

Captain Norrington, fearing it was all the work of pirates, quickly ordered his men to prepare for battle. "Move the boy aft!" he shouted.

"We need to clear the deck!"

Governor Swann pried Elizabeth's hand from the ship's rail and moved her away from the terrible sight. "He's in your charge," he said grimly to her as two sailors moved the boy's body behind the ship's wheel. "You'll watch over him."

Elizabeth nodded to her father. She went and knelt beside the boy as her father hurried away. She brushed his hair gently away from his forehead. The boy's eyes fluttered open.

"My name is Elizabeth Swann," she told him, taking his hand in hers.

"Will Turner," whispered the boy.

"I'm watching over you," she said, trying to comfort him, but the boy slipped back into unconsciousness.

The boy's movements had opened the collar of his shirt, and Elizabeth saw that he was wearing a gold chain with a medallion. She tugged it free from his neck and turned it over in her hand, hoping it might provide her with a clue to his identity. To her amazement, there, etched into the metal, was a skull and crossbones!

"Why, you're a pirate!" she whispered.

Elizabeth quickly hid the medallion under her coat as Captain Norrington passed by.

"Did he speak?" he asked, standing over Will's body.

"His name is Will Turner," she replied. "That's all I found out."

"Very good," said Captain Norrington, and moved on.

When Elizabeth felt sure the captain would not return, she took the gold medallion from her coat to give it one more look. But a sight that left her too frightened to move or cry out suddenly claimed all her attention. Through the fog came a tall ship with great black sails. From its topmost mast it flew a flag – a skull and crossbones! And as the ship slipped back into the fog to escape the cannon fire of the *Dauntless*, the skull on the pirate flag seemed to turn toward Elizabeth and smile.

Chapter 2

At the sound of a loud knock, Elizabeth's eyes suddenly snapped open. She was in her own bed, safe in the governor's mansion. She wondered for a moment if she had been dreaming. Then she turned up the flame of the oil lamp beside her bed and opened the small drawer of her jewellery box. There it was: the gold medallion she had secretly taken from Will Turner's neck eight years ago.

"Still in bed at this hour?" called Governor Swann as he continued to knock on the door.

Elizabeth quickly put on the necklace, threw on her dressing gown and opened the door for her father.

"It's a beautiful day," he announced as he walked in carrying a large box, "and I have a gift for you!"

Elizabeth's maid entered the room behind him and pulled back the heavy curtains, letting in the blue sky and morning light of Port Royal. It was a small, neat town on a snug harbour, guarded by the cannons of Fort Charles, which stood at the edge of the sea.

Governor Swann opened the box and held up an elegant velvet gown. "I thought you could wear it to the ceremony today," he said as Elizabeth, delighted with the gift, took the gown behind a dressing screen. "Captain Norrington's promotion ceremony," he added.

"I knew it," answered Elizabeth, peeking out from behind the screen as her maid tightened her corset strings.

Elizabeth knew that her father favoured a marriage between her and Captain Norrington, but she was in no way interested.

"He is a fine gentleman," her father added, trying to sway her, "and he fancies you, you know."

Elizabeth stepped out from behind the screen and frowned. The dress was beautiful but much too tight. "I'm told it's the latest fashion in London," he said, smiling at his lovely daughter.

"Women in London must have learned not to breathe," commented Elizabeth as she tried to adjust the dress and take a breath.

A while later, Elizabeth was preparing to leave with her father when the butler announced a caller at the door.

Governor Swann descended the stairs to find a young man carrying a long presentation box waiting in the mansion's foyer. It was Will Turner, now a grown man of 20 and a blacksmith by trade.

"Ah, Mr Turner!" said Governor Swann. "It's good to see you again."

"Good day, sir," replied Will. "I have your order."

The governor was very anxious to see the sword that Will had brought him. He opened the box and smiled with satisfaction. The dress sword of gold and steel was going to be presented to Captain Norrington at the ceremony, and Will had done a fine job.

Will began to point out the craftsmanship and balance of the sword to the governor, but as he was doing so, he looked up and saw Elizabeth, who was coming down the stairs. She looked lovelier than ever. A wide smile spread across his face.

"Ah, Elizabeth! You look stunning!" said Governor Swann.

"It's so good to see you," Elizabeth said, greeting Will, her own smile betraying her feelings for the young swordsmith. "I dreamed about you last night. About the day we met. Do you remember?"

"I could never forget, Miss Swann," Will replied.

The direction the conversation was taking obviously did not please Governor Swann. He took the sword from Will and quickly escorted Elizabeth out of the door.

"Good day, Mr Turner," Elizabeth said, smiling once more at her handsome young friend.

She gathered her skirts and stepped into the

waiting carriage with her father. Will stood there watching the carriage until it disappeared into the busy streets of Port Royal.

Chapter
3

On the journey to Fort Charles, Elizabeth could see the HMS *Dauntless* at anchor in the sparkling harbour. It was there to protect the citizens of Port Royal from the threat of thieves and pirates. And in case the presence of the *Dauntless* was not enough to discourage any would-be lawbreakers, the skeletons of four pirates swung from the gallows overlooking the harbour. A fifth noose hung empty, its rope bearing a sign: PIRATES – YE BE WARNED!

The midday sun was blazing hot when Elizabeth and her father arrived at the fort. She truly regretted wearing such a heavy dress in the day's heat. But despite the weather, everyone in town had turned out in their best to see Captain Norrington promoted to the rank of commodore. Elizabeth and her father were escorted to their seats and the ceremony began.

All seemed well . . . but far below the cliff in a small, leaky bit of a boat stood one of the slyest pirates ever to sail the Spanish Main. Captain Jack Sparrow was his name. He gazed solemnly at the pirates' bones that hung from the gallows, and nodded his respects as he sailed by. Then, as he made his way farther into the port, he set his sights on the ships at anchor. Captain Jack had come to Port Royal with a mind to acquire a somewhat larger boat.

He took a long look at the *Dauntless*. And though he knew it was a powerful ship with its 50 guns, Jack's attention was drawn to something very different: the HMS *Interceptor*, a small, sleek vessel with rail guns, and a mortar in the middle of the main deck. It was tied up at the navy landing, below the cliffs of Fort Charles.

Jack never wasted time when he saw something he wanted. Smoothly, he sailed up to the dock.

The harbourmaster looked Jack over. "Hold up there, ye!" he shouted, not liking what he saw of the man or his leaking boat. "The mooring fee's a shilling, and I'll need to know your name."

Jack smiled as the harbourmaster's assistant opened his ledger for Jack to sign. "What do you say to *three* shillings, and we forget the name?" answered Jack, throwing the shillings onto the ledger.

The harbourmaster's expression changed, as though he had completely misjudged Jack. He reached over his assistant's shoulder and closed the ledger with a long, crooked finger. Then he stepped aside and said, "Welcome to Port Royal, *Mr Smith!*"

Giving the harbourmaster a half salute, Jack strapped on his sword and headed up the dock toward the *Interceptor,* smiling. It was turning out to be a fine day, he thought.

He found two sailors guarding the *Interceptor* when he strolled towards its gangplank. "This dock is off limits to civilians," one of the guards warned him.

"Sorry, I didn't know," said Jack as his ear

caught the music of the ceremony taking place at Fort Charles. He shielded his eyes from the bright sun and looked up. "Some sort of to-do at the fort, eh? You two weren't invited?"

"Someone has to make sure this dock is off limits to civilians," the guard answered as he looked at Jack in his tattered pirate's rags.

"Yes," agreed Jack. "That's a fine goal, I'm sure. This must be an important boat."

"*Ship*," snapped the guard. "Commodore Norrington'll use the *Interceptor* to hunt down the last dregs of piracy on the Spanish Lake. There's no ship that can match the *Interceptor* for speed."

"That so?" replied Jack casually. "I've heard of one. Supposed to be fast, nigh uncatchable. The *Black Pearl*?"

Both guards went silent at the mention of the legendary ship.

"There's no *real* ship as can match the *Interceptor*," argued the first guard.

"I've seen it," answered the other. "The *Black Pearl* is a real ship."

The two began to argue over the existence of the notorious *Black Pearl*, and they realized too late that Jack had disappeared from the dock.

"You!" the guard shouted to Jack, who was now standing at the wheel of the *Interceptor*. "Get away from there!"

"I'm sorry," Jack said innocently as the guards charged up the gangplank. "It's just that it's such a pretty boat . . . I mean ship."

"You don't have permission to be aboard! What's your name?" the guard demanded.

"Smith," answered Jack brightly.

"What's your business in Port Royal, Mr Smith? And no lies!"

"None? Very well," sighed Jack. "I confess: I intend to commandeer one of these ships, pick up a crew in Tortuga, go out and do a little honest pirating."

The guards looked confused. "I said no lies!"

"I think he's telling the truth," said the other guard. Meanwhile, Jack noticed a commotion up at the fort. A beautiful girl in a velvet gown was falling from the cliff into the water below!

Chapter
4

Commodore Norrington and Governor Swann leaned over the parapet and considered jumping off the cliff to save Elizabeth, but the dive would have meant certain death. "The rocks, sir! It's a miracle she missed them!" said a soldier, holding Norrington back.

Elizabeth had just been chatting with the commodore. He had told her that now that he had received his promotion, he wished to find a fine woman to be his wife. "You have become a fine woman," he had said, hinting strongly that he wished to marry her.

Elizabeth had gasped and told him she couldn't breathe, but not because of Commodore

Norrington's suggestion that she become his wife. The heat of the midday sun and the tightness of her dress had overcome her, and she had fallen over the wall of the fort in a faint, tumbling towards the water.

Commodore Norrington and Governor Swann rushed down the cliff to the harbour.

Captain Jack Sparrow eyed the whole event impatiently. "Aren't you going to save her?" he asked the two guards as Elizabeth splashed into the water.

Both men looked at Jack blankly. "I can't swim," confessed one. Apparently, neither could the other, who just shook his head.

"Sailors," huffed Jack, resenting the delay in stealing the *Interceptor.* "Fine," he said. He handed his belt and pistol to them. "Don't lose those."

Jack dived into the water and swam towards Elizabeth, who was gasping for air as she disappeared below the surface. She was sinking slowly in the dark water, her velvet gown surrounding her like a cloud, when Jack's arm suddenly grabbed her around the waist.

Jack was a mighty swimmer, but he couldn't bring Elizabeth to the surface. He quickly realized that the weight of Elizabeth's dress was pulling them down. He ripped at the buttons until the heavy, water-soaked dress fell away, and the two of them floated to the surface.

The guards helped Jack haul Elizabeth onto the dock. "She's not breathing," said one of the guards as he put his cheek to her nose and mouth.

"Move," commanded Jack, who suddenly took a knife from the guard's sheath and leaned over Elizabeth.

Then, to the shock of both guards, Jack took the blade and slit Elizabeth's corset down the middle. Elizabeth immediately began coughing and sputtering.

"I never would have thought of that," said the guard.

"Clearly you've never been to Singapore," said Jack with a devilish smile. He was about to ask Elizabeth how she was feeling when he suddenly felt a blade at his neck.

"On your feet!" said Commodore Norrington to Jack. The pirate thought of trying to explain his position, but he knew it looked bad.

"Elizabeth! Are you all right?" asked Governor Swann.

"Yes, yes, I'm fine," Elizabeth said to her father.

As Captain Norrington tightened his grip on Jack, he noticed a brand on the stranger's inner wrist: the letter *P*, and above it, a tattoo of a small bird in flight across water. "Well, well . . . a pirate," remarked Norrington. "Jack Sparrow, isn't it?" Norrington's guards drew their pistols.

"*Captain* Jack Sparrow, if you please," answered Jack.

"I don't see your ship . . . *Captain*," Commodore Norrington sneered.

"He said he'd come to commandeer one," said one of the guards, handing over Jack's belt and pistol. Norrington examined the pirate's possessions and snorted. He was unimpressed with Jack's pistol, which held only a single shot, and his compass, which didn't point north.

"You are without a doubt the worst pirate I have ever heard of," Norrington taunted.

"Ah, but you have heard of me," Jack said, smiling.

Norrington had seen enough of the man by now to know that he would hang him in the morning, along with whatever other pirates were in prison at Fort Charles. "Fetch some irons," he said in a flat tone.

"I must protest," Elizabeth said. "Pirate or not, this man saved my life!" But Commodore Norrington wasn't about to let Jack get away. The guards fastened manacles around Jack's wrists.

"Finally . . ." sighed Jack, and lightning-quick snapped the corset he still held. Its laces caught around the pistol in the guard's hand and sent it sailing into the water. The men were momentarily shocked as Jack wrapped the chain between his manacles tightly around Elizabeth's neck. The pistol of every sailor on the dock now pointed at Jack, but Commodore Norrington raised his hand to hold his troops back. Jack was using Elizabeth as a shield. Commodore Norrington feared she might be killed.

Jack ordered Elizabeth to grab his belt and pistol and began backing them down the dock. "You are despicable!" Elizabeth said as she struggled.

But Jack only smiled. "I saved your life; now you've saved mine," he said. "We're square."

Then Jack announced, "Gentlemen. M'lady. You will always remember this as the day you *almost* caught Jack Sparrow." And with that, he shoved Elizabeth away, grabbed a ship's rope, and swung high and wide. Captain Norrington carefully aimed his pistol at Jack and fired. His bullet hit the rope, and Jack fell from high in the rigging.

Jack tumbled, then snapped the manacle chain over a line and slid down it to the deck of the ship. In an instant, Jack jumped from the deck . . . and dashed away.

"On his heels!" shouted Norrington. A squad of sailors took off into the streets and alleys of Port Royal. The hunt for Jack Sparrow was on!

Now standing alone on the dock with his daughter, Governor Swann placed his coat around Elizabeth's shoulders. The air had suddenly grown cold, and a thick fog from the harbour began to gather at their feet.

Chapter
5

The search party moved cautiously down a narrow alleyway. The fog had rolled in, making it difficult to see. They looked everywhere, but there was no sign of the pirate.

Jack slipped out from his hiding place behind a large statue once he was sure the search party had passed. As he crept along, he tested the doors of a darkened blacksmith's shop. He smiled as the double doors slid easily open.

The forge was dark, lit by only a few lanterns. Jack could see that the walls were covered with chains and tools. He was about to thank his luck for the chance to use them to cut the manacles from his wrists when he was startled by a loud snort. In the corner, drunk and asleep, was Mr Brown, the blacksmith. Jack tiptoed over and poked him hard. But Mr Brown didn't move, he just snorted loudly again.

Satisfied that the man would cause him no trouble, Jack walked over to the furnace and lowered the chain between his wrists into the hot coals. When the chain began to glow red, Jack took a short-handled sledgehammer from the wall and with one hard stroke broke the manacle from one wrist. His arm was red and blistered, but his hands were finally free.

Jack was about to break the manacle from his other wrist when he heard the iron latch on the door move. Quickly, he dived for cover just as Will Turner stepped into the blacksmith's shop.

Will looked around the forge and saw old Mr Brown asleep in the corner. "Right where I left you," muttered Will. Then he looked at the sledgehammer lying on the furnace and said, "Hmm, not where I left you." Will was reaching to pick up the sledgehammer and put it in its proper place when a blade suddenly came out of the darkness and slapped his hand!

Will jumped back and came face to face with Jack Sparrow, who now had his sword levelled at Will's chest. Will looked him over from head to toe. "Why, you're the one they're hunting," he said, glaring at Jack. "The pirate!"

Will grabbed a sword lying next to the furnace and pointed it at Jack.

"Do you think this is wise, boy? Crossing swords with a pirate?" asked Jack. He was unhappy to see Will answer the question by raising his sword in attack.

Will and Jack thrust and cut at each other with lightning speed. "You know what you're doing, I'll give you that," said Jack as the two circled each other, Will keeping up with every move Jack made.

Jack moved until the door of the forge was at his back. Then, to Will's surprise, the pirate turned and made a run for it. Will reacted in an instant and threw his sword at Jack's back.

The sword flew over Jack's head and buried itself deep in the planks of the door. Jack pulled on the latch, but it was no good. The sword was in the way.

Will thought he had his opponent trapped. But Jack Sparrow always had another plan in his pocket. Slowly, he turned to Will and smiled.

Jack was now eyeing the back door of the blacksmith's shop. "That's a good trick. Except, once again, you are between me and the way out," he said, pointing his sword at the back door. "And now," he added confidently, "you have no weapon!"

Will simply took another sword from the rack and began to attack.

As Jack parried, he looked around and noticed that the shop was filled with weapons. "Who makes all these?" he asked.

"I do," Will answered as their swords clashed and rang again. "And I practise with them three hours a day!"

"You need to find yourself a girl . . . or maybe the reason you practise three hours a day is you've found one but can't get her?" Jack teased.

"I practise three hours a day so when I meet a pirate, I can kill him!" Will answered angrily, and pushed his sword against Jack until the pirate's back was against the wall.

Jack swung the chain on his wrist around Will's sword and tried to pull it free. But Will was quick. He twisted the point of his sword through a link and stabbed it into the ceiling, leaving Jack hanging by his manacled wrist.

Jack kept fighting with one hand as he hung from the ceiling. He twisted around and compressed the furnace bellows with his foot. A shower of sparks flew into the air and hit Will in the face. Will stepped back and covered his eyes.

Jack used his full weight to yank the sword free from the ceiling. Then, dropping to the floor, he grabbed a mallet and hurled it at Will, smashing the boy's wrist. Will dropped his sword and fell. When he got up, Jack's pistol was aimed right between his eyes.

"You cheated!" Will shouted. Jack raised his eyebrows and smiled, as if to say, 'What do you expect from a pirate?'.

"You're lucky, boy," Jack told him, and motioned him away from the door. "This shot's not meant for you."

Jack was moving to make his escape when Mr Brown suddenly came out from a corner and slammed his bottle against Jack's skull.

Jack crumpled to the floor as the doors of the forge flew open and armed sailors rushed into the room. Commodore Norrington pushed his way to the front of the crowd. "Excellent work, Mr Brown," said Norrington, standing over Jack. "I believe you will always remember this as the day Captain Jack Sparrow *almost* escaped!"

As Norrington's men hauled Jack away, Mr Brown looked at the broken glass on the floor and sadly said, "That rotter broke my bottle!"

Chapter
6

Night fell, and the thick fog now blanketed the entire town of Port Royal. Only Fort Charles, high on a cliff, could be seen above the grey mist. But out in the harbour, cutting through the fog like a shark's fin, was the topmast of a tall, black ship flying the skull and crossbones. . . .

The fog brought a strange uneasiness with it. Elizabeth, cosy in her bed, was trying to read herself to sleep – but suddenly, the flame of her lamp flickered, then went out. She tried to turn it up, but it wouldn't work . . . the room was black.

In the blacksmith's shop, Will thought he heard a strange noise. He took an axe from the wall and stepped outside to look down the alley . . . but everything in the mist was still and silent.

Only Jack Sparrow, now stuck in a prison cell, had no fear of what might be lurking in the fog.

Jack's cell was next to that of three prisoners who were to be hanged along with him in the morning. The three had spent hours trying to coax a mangy dog with a ring of keys in its mouth over to their cell.

"You can keep doing that forever," Jack sighed as they waggled a bone at the dog. "That dog is never going to move."

"Excuse us if we ain't resigned ourselves to go to the gallows just yet," answered one of the prisoners, holding a loop of rope he hoped to land around the dog's neck. But Jack sat back and hoped for better things.

Commodore Norrington and Governor Swann were walking along the parapet overlooking the gallows when the sudden boom of cannon fire knocked them both off their feet. The explosion rocked the jail cell, too, sending Jack and his new-found friends running to the window. "I know those guns!" shouted Jack through the bars of his cell. "It's the *Black Pearl!*"

The fog lit up around the *Black Pearl* each time it fired its cannons on the town. Whole streets, buildings and docks exploded into bits. The citizens of Port Royal ran in horror. Then, out of the fog and smoke, came longboats loaded with pirates. Swarming ashore, the mob quickly overtook the town, running through the streets, setting fires and murdering any poor soul not quick enough to get away.

Will Turner armed himself with everything he could carry. He grabbed sabres, knives and a heavy broadaxe. The brash young blacksmith boldly headed up the street. A woman being chased by a pirate ran screaming past him. He backhanded the pirate square in the chest with the broad side of his axe and continued up the street.

Wiping dust and smoke from his eyes, Will looked up towards the governor's mansion. There, against the light of the moon, he saw the silhouettes of two pirates heading for the doors of the mansion. *Elizabeth!* he thought – but before he could act, pirates struck him from behind.

Chapter 7

A loud banging sent Elizabeth running to her window. She looked down and saw two brutes with their fists raised. She dashed from her room and reached the top of the mansion's staircase just as the butler opened the door. It was too late to warn him!

The two filthy pirates, one named Pintel and the other Ragetti, stormed into the room. The taller of the two, Ragetti, had a wooden eye that squeaked when it moved. They were each armed with a cutlass and pistol, shining and ready for use.

Elizabeth almost fainted when she heard the boom of the pirate's gun. The butler crumpled to the floor and the pirate holding the smoking pistol looked up at Elizabeth and smiled.

Terrified, Elizabeth ran to her room and locked the door as the two pirates charged up the stairs. Suddenly, a body slammed hard against the door, shaking it to its hinges. Elizabeth grabbed a bed warmer filled with hot coals and hit Pintel with it squarely in the face as he broke through the door. He staggered back, holding his burning, broken nose.

Elizabeth swung again as Ragetti rushed through the doorway. This time, the hot coals of the bed warmer spilled sizzling onto Ragetti's head, setting his hair and wooden eye on fire. Elizabeth ran for the hallway stairs.

The pirates burst from the bedroom, furious. They saw Elizabeth trying to escape down the stairs. In an instant, Ragetti vaulted over the banister to stop her. Behind her, Pintel was flying down the stairs. Ragetti landed in front of her, his hair and wooden eye still smouldering. She was trapped!

Suddenly, the wall of the mansion exploded as a cannonball ripped through the foyer. A chandelier came crashing to the floor, causing both pirates to take cover.

Elizabeth raced into the dining room and bolted the doors behind her. *If I could only find a weapon*, she thought as she frantically looked through the room. There was nothing. Knowing the pirates would break the doors down at any moment, she dived into a linen closet and hid.

Elizabeth held her breath, then cringed when she heard the pirates rush into the room. "We know you're here, poppet. Come out and we promise we won't hurt you," said Pintel, winking at his smouldering friend. "We will find you," he continued. "You've got something of ours, and it calls to us. The gold calls to us."

Elizabeth shrank back against the linen-laden shelves and looked down at the medallion around her neck. Light through a crack in the door glinted on the gold for an instant, then disappeared. Elizabeth looked up to see what was blocking the light and saw Pintel's eye glaring at her.

"Hello, poppet . . ."

Chapter
8

Ah, but it was shaping up to be a fine day, Jack Sparrow thought from his cell. The jail was being blown to bits around him, and with every boom of the *Black Pearl*'s cannons, Jack knew he was that much closer to freedom.

But while cannonballs exploded throughout the prison, not one came through Jack's cell. "My sympathies, friend," said one of the prisoners from the next cell as the three made their escape through the rubble. "You've no manner of luck at all."

Jack had to agree as he watched them climb to the rocks below . . . and to freedom. He sat in his prison cell alone. The moon was just beginning to rise above the fog, and the *Black Pearl's* guns were firing in another direction.

Jack breathed a deep sigh, then looked around the battered prison and noticed the dog cowering under a long bench. The keys were still in its mouth. *What the heck*, thought Jack, and he reached into the next cell, picked up the old bone and said, "Here, doggie."

To his utter surprise, the dog got up! It moved closer and closer until the keys were almost in Jack's hand. But the dog became nervous. It started to whine, then stopped. "What's the matter, boy?" Jack asked. Just then the prison door slammed open and the dog bolted.

Two pirates from the *Black Pearl* swaggered in. "This isn't the armoury," one said to the other as they looked around. One of the pirates spotted Jack in the cell. "Well, well . . . look what we have here. It's Captain Sparrow."

"Last time we saw you, you were all alone on a godforsaken island," said the other. "How the devil did you get off . . . sprout little wings and fly?" The pirates laughed. "Your fortunes aren't improved much!"

"Worry about your own fortunes. The deepest circles of hell are for betrayers and mutineers!" snarled Jack fiercely. Not liking Jack's answer much, one of the pirates reached through the bars and grabbed him by the throat. Jack clutched at the pirate's arms and tried to wrestle free. But when he looked down, he saw that he wasn't holding arms at all. In the moonlight he saw nothing but the bare bones of a skeleton in his hands.

"There *is* a curse!" declared Jack, and the pirate snapped his hands back out of the light. Seeing the bones turn back to human flesh, Jack said, "So the stories *are* true!"

"You know nothing of hell," one of the pirates said. Then they turned their backs on him and walked out.

Chapter
9

Amid the thunder of cannon fire, a longboat piled high with loot slipped through the fog and out into the harbour. Elizabeth sat in the prow, terrified, as the pirates rowed the longboat towards the dark, massive hull of their ship.

As they rowed closer, Elizabeth could see on the bow an ornately carved figurehead of a woman with a small bird in her outstretched hand. Then she looked up as the fog parted. Looming high above her were yards and yards of black canvas. She was under the sails of the *Black Pearl*.

Smoke hung heavy on the lantern-lit deck as the longboat was raised to the rails. Elizabeth could see that the pirate crew had been mustered from many parts of the world. The heads of several were covered with knotted kerchiefs. Some wore silk waistcoats and ruffled capes, no doubt looted from some luckless ship that now sat wasted and rotting at the bottom of the sea. All were sunburned, savage men, and all had their eyes on Elizabeth!

"She's invoked the right of *parley* with Captain Barbossa," announced Pintel, pushing her onto the deck. The pirates were silent. Even cutthroats had a code of honour. The right of parley would protect any prisoner until he or she had had an audience with the captain.

Then, as if someone had spoken of the devil himself, the dark figure of a man slowly stepped out of the smoke and onto the main deck. It was the captain of the *Black Pearl* – Barbossa. A monkey jumped out of the rigging and landed on his shoulder, scaring Elizabeth senseless.

Barbossa stepped forward and Elizabeth tried to speak, but Bo'sun slapped her hard. "You'll speak when spoken to!" he hissed.

"And *you'll* not lay a hand on those under the protection of parley!" growled the captain, grabbing Bo'sun's wrist. "My apologies, miss," he said, turning to Elizabeth.

"I have come to negotiate the cessation of hostilities against Port Royal," she said, trying to appear confident.

Captain Barbossa smiled like the amused father of a small child. "There was a lot of long words in there, miss, and we're naught but humble pirates. What is it you want?"

"I want you to leave and never come back," Elizabeth answered firmly.

The crew laughed. Captain Barbossa told her that that would simply not be possible.

"Very well," said Elizabeth, running to the rail and dangling the gold medallion over the side. "I'll drop it!"

The crew suddenly went quiet. "I know it's what you're searching for," she said. "I recognize this ship. I saw it eight years ago."

"Did you, now?" said the captain, who didn't seem to care a rap about what Elizabeth had to say.

"Fine," said Elizabeth, flipping the medallion into the air. "Then there's no reason to keep it!"

The monkey screeched.

"No!" shouted Barbossa.

Elizabeth caught the medallion by its chain and smiled triumphantly.

Barbossa stepped back and took a long look at Elizabeth. "You have a name, missy?" he asked.

Elizabeth tried to think quickly. She was afraid things would be worse for her if they knew she was the governor's daughter, so she said, "Elizabeth. Elizabeth Turner." The pirates gave one another sidelong glances. "I'm a maid in the governor's household."

"Very well." Barbossa nodded. "Hand that over; we'll put your town to our rudder and ne'er return."

Elizabeth was thrilled that he would agree to leave. "Can I trust you?" she asked.

Captain Barbossa raised his voice and warned her, "Hand it over now, or these be the last friendly words you'll hear!"

Elizabeth had no choice. She held out the medallion. Bo'sun reached for it, but the monkey grabbed it first and took it to Barbossa.

"Our bargain?" asked Elizabeth anxiously.

Barbossa smiled and told Bo'sun to still the

guns. "Signal the men and make good to clear port."

Elizabeth was relieved to hear the cannon fire finally stop. Then she realized that the ship was leaving. "Wait!" she said. "You must return me to shore. According to the rules of order . . ."

Captain Barbossa wheeled around.

"First, your return to shore was not part of our negotiations nor our agreement, and so I must do nothing. Secondly, you must be a pirate for the pirates' code to apply. And thirdly," he said, smiling with teeth of gleaming gold and silver, "the code is more what you'd call guidelines than actual rules. Welcome aboard the *Black Pearl*, Miss Turner!"

Chapter
10

After the cannon fire stopped, the fog slowly lifted, revealing a harbour full of sunken and burning ships. Will Turner struggled to his feet and rubbed the bump on his head as he looked at the destruction. He thought only of Elizabeth as he raced to Fort Charles.

"They've taken her!" he shouted as he burst into Commodore Norrington's office.

Norrington and Governor Swann looked up for a moment from the map of the Caribbean draped over the desk; then Norrington turned to one of the two guards by the door. "Mr Murtogg, remove this man from my office."

Murtogg grabbed Will by the arm, but Will shook him off.

Norrington looked up impatiently. "Mr Turner, you are not a military man, you are not a sailor – you are a blacksmith. You have nothing of value to contribute here. And this is not a time for rash actions," he said.

"We have to hunt them down," Will protested, "and save her!"

"We'll launch a search mission on the next tide," Norrington said, looking back at his map.

Commodore Norrington and the governor were trying to calculate where the *Black Pearl* might be headed when Murtogg remembered something he'd heard: "That Jack Sparrow . . . he talked about the *Black Pearl*."

"Mentioned it, is more what he did," said the other guard.

"Ask him where it is!" demanded Will, knowing they were wasting precious time. "Make a deal with him! He can lead us to it!"

But Norrington refused. "Leave, Mr Turner!"

Will stormed out of the office and headed for the prison to speak to Jack Sparrow himself.

Jack was trying his luck at removing the bars of his cell when Will raced through the prison doors.

"You. Sparrow. Are you familiar with that ship . . . the *Black Pearl?*"

"Somewhat," answered Jack calmly.

"Where does it make berth?" Will demanded.

"The *Black Pearl* sails from the dreaded Isla de la Muerta. Surely you've heard the stories," answered Jack. "But why ask me?"

"They took Miss Swann," said Will, clenching his fists.

"Ah, so it *is* you found a girl," Jack said knowingly, ". . . but I see no profit in it for me."

Will pulled a bench up to Jack's cell. "I could get you out of here," he offered.

Jack looked into Will's face. "What's your name, boy?" he asked.

"Will Turner."

Jack smiled and nodded. "Well, Mr Turner, tell you what. I've changed my mind. You spring me from this cell, and I'll take you to the *Black Pearl*. Do we have an accord?" he asked, sticking his hand through the bars.

"Agreed!" said Will, and shook the pirate's hand firmly.

It was morning when Jack and Will made their way down to the dock. The *Dauntless* was still at anchor in the harbour.

"We're going to steal *that* ship?" asked Will, pointing to the *Dauntless*.

"Commandeer," said Jack, correcting him. "We're going to *commandeer* that ship . . . nautical term."

Jack led Will to an overturned rowing boat, and they both climbed under it. Jack instructed Will to raise the rowing boat to shoulder height. Then the two began walking toward the water, zigzagging along the beach like a crab.

"This is either brilliant or crazy," Will said as they walked into the water.

"Remarkable how often those two traits coincide," answered Jack.

They had tied bags of sand around the rowing boat for ballast. Safely breathing the air that was trapped in the rowing boat's hull, the two men moved closer and closer to the ship.

The racket of sailors aboard ship went silent when Jack and Will suddenly jumped over the rail of the *Dauntless*. "Everybody stay calm," announced Jack, brandishing a pistol. "We're taking over the ship!"

The crew looked at Jack, then at Will – and burst out laughing. "This ship cannot be crewed by two men!" said one of the sailors. "You'll never make it out of the bay!"

But the prediction didn't worry Jack. "I've never been one to resist a challenge," he said, motioning with his pistol for the crew to climb into the rowing boat.

In the meantime, aboard Norrington's ship, the *Interceptor*, the crew was setting up the rigging. The commodore was readying to make sail and hunt down the *Black Pearl*. From the *Interceptor*'s deck, Norrington noticed that the *Dauntless* seemed to be moving. He took out his spyglass for a closer look. Sure enough, it was sailing out of the harbour! He then recognized Will on the main deck and Jack Sparrow at the wheel – the *Dauntless* was now theirs!

Chapter
11

Norrington couldn't believe his eyes! Jack Sparrow was trying to commandeer the *Dauntless*! Norrington knew that the *Interceptor* was faster than the *Dauntless*, and with only Jack and Will to sail the *Dauntless*, he'd catch them in no time! He gave his crew the order and they took off full sail.

"Here they come!" Will shouted to Jack.

As the *Interceptor* drew up alongside its quarry, Norrington found the decks of the *Dauntless* empty. "Search every cabin, every hold, down to the bilges!" he commanded as the entire crew of the *Interceptor* boarded the *Dauntless*.

But that left the *Interceptor* empty except for one lone sentry. In a flash, Jack and Will climbed over the rail unseen. The *Interceptor* was theirs!

"Can you swim?" Jack asked the sentry, grabbing the man's neck.

"Like a fish . . . " the sentry promised.

"Good," said Jack, and threw him overboard.

Jack and Will quickly threw off the ropes that held the two ships together and raised the foresail.

Seeing the *Interceptor* move away, Norrington shouted to his crew to turn the *Dauntless* and man the cannons. But it was too late. Jack had cut the rudder chain of the *Dauntless*, leaving it in his wake. The *Interceptor* was sailing into the horizon to find the *Black Pearl*, with Jack Sparrow at the wheel.

Locked in a cabin aboard the *Black Pearl*, Elizabeth was startled when two pirates barged through the door. They were the same two who had taken her from the mansion, Pintel and his one-eyed friend, Ragetti.

"You'll be dining with the captain. He requests you wear this," said Pintel, shoving a black silk dress toward her. The two turned and left Elizabeth to change. She was examining the dress when she heard a loud squeak coming from the door. The pirates were peeking through the keyhole!

Elizabeth took a hairpin, pushed it through the keyhole, and felt it hit something hard and wooden. "Ow! Me eye!" howled Ragetti. The hairpin plucked the wooden eye from his head and sent it rolling down the deck.

"Don't let it drown!" he yelled, and went scrambling after it. The eye rolled to a stop under the boot of Bo'sun, who said, "I'd be happy to nail it in place for ya!" and kicked it down the deck. Every pirate aboard roared with laughter as they stomped past the one-eyed pirate, who was now bumping around the deck on his hands and knees.

In Captain Barbossa's cabin, a huge feast was laid out on the table. Elizabeth wore the black silk dress and watched Captain Barbossa enter the cabin with the monkey on his shoulder.

"You must be hungry," he told her, motioning to the meat and bread on the table. "Please . . . dig in."

Elizabeth was starving. She tore off a large piece of bread and took a bite. "Try the wine," the captain said with fierce delight, "and the apples . . . one of those next."

Elizabeth stopped for a second and realized the captain was watching her put the food into her mouth and chew – so were all the pirates . . . so was the monkey!

Thinking the food was poisoned, Elizabeth panicked.

"You eat it!" she cried.

"Would that I could," replied the captain, looking at the feast in front of him. He knew there wasn't a man on board who could take a bite and taste it. He took the gold medallion from his pocket and dangled it from his finger.

"This is Aztec gold," he said, falling into a sombre mood. "One of 882 identical pieces delivered in a stone chest to Cortés himself. Blood money, Miss Turner. . . . And so the heathen gods placed upon the gold a terrible curse."

"I hardly believe in ghost stories," Elizabeth said.

Captain Barbossa shook his head. "Aye, that's exactly what I thought when first we were told the tale!

"Buried on an Island of the Dead," Barbossa recalled, "find it we did. And there be the chest, and inside be the coins . . . and we took 'em all. Spent 'em and traded 'em for drink and food and pleasant company. But the more we gave 'em away, the more we came to realize: the drink would not satisfy, and the food turned to ash in our mouths. We are cursed men, Miss Turner. Compelled by greed we were, but now we are consumed by it."

Barbossa placed a consoling hand on the monkey, which whimpered as his master told the tale.

"But there is one way to end the curse," Barbossa said, raising an eyebrow. "All the scattered pieces of the Aztec gold must be restored . . . and the blood repaid.

"Ten years we searched, looting ship and port, sifting through our plunder for it all!" He looked at the medallion lovingly. "And now, thanks to you, we have the final piece. Once we've reunited it with its mates, we are free."

Elizabeth thought for a moment. "And the blood to be repaid?" she asked. "What of it?"

Barbossa looked at her and smiled. "Apple?" he asked her. Elizabeth was stunned. She suddenly realized that it was her blood he wanted.

Horrified, Elizabeth bolted out of her chair. She struggled for a moment with Captain Barbossa, then reached for a table knife and plunged it into his chest. The captain calmly looked at the wound, and to Elizabeth's shock, no blood came from it.

Terrified, Elizabeth ran from the cabin to the deck of the ship. There in the moonlight she saw the crew of the *Black Pearl* at work and froze. She shut her eyes tightly.

Captain Barbossa came up on deck and grabbed her. "Look!" he shouted. "The moonlight shows us for what we really are!"

Elizabeth opened her eyes and saw the pirates

at their stations, coiling the lines and raising the black sails. They sang an old sea shanty as they worked, but where the moonlight fell across their bodies, Elizabeth saw nothing but the bones of skeletons!

The skeletal monkey, holding the medallion, shrieked and jumped onto Captain Barbossa's shoulder. "We are not among the living," Barbossa said as two skeletons played a pirate tune, "and so we cannot die!" He leaned into the moonlight, turning his face into a fleshless skull.

The captain took a bottle of wine from an open case by the cabin door and uncorked it with his teeth. He raised it as if in a toast to Elizabeth.

"You'd best start believing in ghost stories, Miss Turner," Barbossa advised as he drank straight from the bottle, the wine gushing out from between his empty ribs. "You're in one."

Chapter
12

The *Interceptor* was as fast as Jack had hoped, and with a favouring wind it could log a fair distance in a day's run. Jack reckoned they were now only a few miles from Tortuga, where he knew he could find himself an able crew.

Jack was surprised at how quickly Will had taken to being a sailor. "I worked passage from England as a cabin boy," Will explained. "After my mother passed, I came out here looking for my father . . . Bill Turner."

"That so?" asked Jack slyly.

"You knew my father," Will said to Jack. "It was only after you learned my name at the jail that you agreed to help."

Jack sighed and considered what story he might tell Will, but then decided to tell him the truth. "I knew him," he said. "Most everyone just called him Bill . . . Bootstrap Bill."

"Bootstrap?" said Will, surprised.

"Good man," answered Jack. "Good pirate."

Will looked shocked. "It's not true that my father was a pirate!" he declared. "He was a merchant marine! A respectable man who obeyed the law!"

"Ah, there's quite a few who come out here hoping to amass enough swag to ease the burdens of respectable life . . . and they're all merchant marines," said Jack with a knowing smile.

"My father did not think of his family as a burden!" argued Will.

"Sure, because he could always go pirating!" Jack said.

"My father was not a pirate!" exclaimed Will, pulling out his sword.

"Put it away," Jack said to Will in a dull voice. "It's not worth getting beat again." When Jack saw that Will was going to push the point, he turned the wheel of the *Interceptor* hard, and the boom whipped around and struck Will in the chest.

Will held on as the boom carried him out over the foaming sea. "As long as you're just hanging there," said Jack, picking up Will's sword, "pay attention. You can accept that your father was a pirate and still a good man – or you can't. Now me, I can let you drown . . . but I can't land this ship at Tortuga without your help."

A wave came up and almost cost Will his grip. "So . . . " Jack said, pointing the sword at Will, "can you sail under the command of a pirate or not?"

With the island of Tortuga lying dead ahead and Jack's sword pointing at him, Will agreed. Jack swung the boom around, and Will set his feet back on the deck. Then Jack handed him his sword and smiled.

Together, they trimmed the forward jib and readied the mooring lines. The *Interceptor* would soon arrive in Tortuga.

Chapter
13

Jack stepped ashore, happy to be in a port that felt like home. A woman with red hair and a redder dress walked up to Jack. "Scarlett!" exclaimed Jack, putting out his arms. She slapped his face and stalked off.

"I didn't deserve that," said Jack. Will raised an eyebrow but didn't say a word.

Tortuga was a dank, dirty port where the tides had swept together the scum of the Caribbean, and Jack Sparrow loved it all. He could hear the laughter of drunken pirates as they chased women through the streets and dunked a merchant just for sport.

"What do you think?" Jack asked as a woman

dumped a chamber pot from a window above them.

"It'll linger," answered Will, turning his head to avoid the stench.

"Aye, unforgettable," agreed Jack, not noticing Will's distaste. "I tell you, Will, if every town in the world was like this one, no man would ever feel unwanted!"

A blonde young lady stepped up to Jack. "Giselle!" exclaimed Jack with a smile. She smiled back, slapped him hard and walked on.

"I didn't deserve that, either," said Jack, rubbing his face.

"How many women are there in this town?" asked Will, worrying for Jack's future.

"You're right," said Jack after a moment's thought. "The quicker we get our crew and away, the better! And here's where we'll find our quartermaster," he said, pointing to a tavern called The Faithful Bride.

Will looked up at a hanging sign that showed a bride holding a bouquet of flowers, her wrists manacled and chained. "This way!" said Jack, leading Will around to the back of the tavern.

Lying in the mud with two pigs behind the tavern was old Joshaemee Gibbs. *Drunk, as usual,* thought Jack as he threw a bucket of water over Gibbs's face.

"Curse you for breathing!" sputtered Gibbs – then he opened his eyes and saw Jack's face.

Jack was helping his old friend to his feet when Will doused the man with another bucket of water. "Blast it, I'm already awake!" Gibbs yelled.

"That was for the smell," Will said as Jack helped Gibbs stumble into the tavern.

Jack and Gibbs sat in a dark corner of The Faithful Bride while Will kept a lookout at the door. Their table was lit by a single candle, and they leaned in close so as not to be heard. "I'm going after the *Black Pearl*," whispered Jack. Gibbs straightened up.

"It's a fool's errand," he told Jack. "Why, you know better than me the tales of the *Black Pearl!*"

"Then it's a good thing I'm not a fool," replied Jack, raising his glass with a grin.

Gibbs was not convinced. "Prove me wrong," he said. "What makes you think Barbossa will give up the *Black Pearl* to you?"

"I've got the right leverage," Jack answered, jerking his head toward Will, who stood at the door out of earshot.

"The kid?"

"That is the child of Bootstrap Bill Turner. His *only* child!" whispered Jack.

Gibbs looked over at Will, who was trying to keep some scoundrel from chasing a serving wench, then narrowed his eyes. "Leverage, say you. I think I feel a change in the wind, says I. I'll find us a crew!" he said excitedly, and slammed his tankard down on the table.

By morning, Gibbs had lined up every weather-beaten, ragged rogue in Tortuga for Jack's inspection. "Feast your eyes, Cap'n. All of them faithful hands before the mast. Every man worth his salt, and crazy to boot!"

Jack moved down the line. It was a motley crew of men, some of whom looked like they hadn't seen a patch of good luck in a good, long time. He passed several, then came upon a bright-eyed prospect with a large, colourful parrot on his shoulder. Jack looked at him and raised an eyebrow . . . but the sailor said nothing.

"Cotton here is mute, sir. Poor devil had his tongue cut out," said Gibbs, opening up Cotton's mouth. Jack cringed. "So he went and trained the parrot to talk for him," Gibbs continued brightly.

"Wind in your sails!" screeched the parrot.

Jack sighed, nodded, and continued on. He stopped in front of a hunched sailor whose face was shaded by a three-cornered hat. Jack leaned over to get a closer look and was suddenly slapped to the ground. The hat fell away and there stood a woman as strong and tall as Jack.

"Guess you didn't deserve that one, either?" asked Will.

"No, that one I deserved," answered Jack. "Hello, AnaMaria."

"You stole my boat!" she shouted.

"Borrowed," said Jack. "Without permission – but with every intention of bringing it back!"

"And did you bring it back?" AnaMaria demanded.

"Ah . . . no, but I've got something better," answered Jack, motioning to the *Interceptor*.

Jack looked at the line of men. "I'm asking all of you to join my crew," he announced. "Sail under my command, and at voyage's end, the *Interceptor* will be yours! What do you say?"

The sailors nodded enthusiastically. "Aye! I'm in!" they shouted.

"You can get your assignments from my first mate," Jack said, and nodded to AnaMaria. "Prepare to set sail!"

The crew poured onto the *Interceptor* immediately and the ship left Tortuga within the hour.

Chapter
14

Far out over the Caribbean Sea, thunder cracked. The *Interceptor* pitched from side to side as it headed into the dark clouds of a great storm. Jack stood at the ship's bow, looked at his compass and nodded. Things were going well, he thought. Again he looked at his compass, which never pointed to true north but always pointed the way to Isla de la Muerta, berth of the *Black Pearl*.

The ship tilted in the high seas and howling wind, the white canvas of its sails stretched tight.

"We'd best drop the canvas, sir!" shouted Gibbs, fearing that the sails might come apart.

"She can hold a bit longer," answered Jack as

the storm gained force. The wind picked up speed, roaring through the ship. Jack looked at his compass, then out to sea. He smiled.

"What's in your head as puts you in such a fine mood, Captain?" shouted Gibbs over the wind.

"We're catching up!" answered Jack.

In the meantime, on the deck of the *Black Pearl*, Elizabeth was being bound and gagged by Pintel.

"Time to go, poppet," he said with a smirk, yanking the ropes at her wrist. She tried to jerk away as Captain Barbossa was draping the gold medallion around her neck, but it did her no good. He tilted her head to judge the look of it and smiled.

Elizabeth was placed in a longboat laden with treasure, one of several that began to row from the *Black Pearl*. As they passed out of the fog, Elizabeth could see a dark sea cave looming ahead. The longboats glided into the cave and were swallowed by the darkness. They had arrived on the dreaded Isla de la Muerta.

Chapter
15

"Dead men tell no tales!" squawked Cotton's parrot as the *Interceptor* slowly slipped into the fog surrounding the island. The crew was watchful and tense.

Suddenly, as the ship emerged from the dense fog, there came a low scraping sound from below. Will looked around to find that they had sailed into a graveyard of the many ships that had been dashed on the reefs surrounding Isla de la Muerta. It was the mast of one such ship that now scraped the bottom of the *Interceptor* and threatened to take her under.

Jack was at the wheel. He quickly snapped his compass shut and concentrated on navigating through the graveyard. He made a few small corrections and the scraping stopped. Gibbs and Will stared at the grey bones of the dead ships as the *Interceptor* slowly glided past.

"Where'd he get that compass?" Will whispered.

"Told me once he served as apprentice to a cartographer for a time," Gibbs answered. "But I can't say . . . only heard he showed up in Tortuga one night with a notion to go for the treasure of Isla de la Muerta. This was when he was captain of the *Black Pearl*."

"What?" said Will, surprised to hear that the *Black Pearl* had once belonged to Jack Sparrow.

Will leaned in closer to hear the tale. "Ah, but Jack Sparrow has an honest streak in him. That's where all his problems start," Gibbs lamented.

Gibbs explained that Jack had promised each member of the crew an equal share of treasure. Shaking his head, Gibbs said, "So his first mate come to him and says if everything's an equal share, that should mean the location of the treasure, too. So Jack gave up the bearings.

"That night, there was mutiny," Gibbs said sadly. "They marooned Jack on an island and left him there to die.

"Now, when a pirate's marooned, he's given a pistol with a single shot. After three weeks of a starving belly and thirst, that pistol starts to look real friendly," Gibbs said, putting his finger to his head to demonstrate for Will.

"But Jack – he survived!" exclaimed Gibbs. "And he still has that single shot. He won't use it, though, save on one man. His mutinous first mate . . ."

"Barbossa!" said Will, seeing the pieces fall into place.

"Aye."

"But how did Jack get off the island?" asked Will.

"He roped himself some sea turtles, lashed 'em together, and made a raft," said the old sailor with a firm nod.

"Sea turtles?" asked Will, unbelieving.

"Aye," Gibbs said earnestly; then Jack suddenly ordered his crew to drop anchor and lower the rowing boat.

"Will and I are going ashore," he announced.

"Aye, Captain," answered AnaMaria.

Gibbs leaned in close to Jack. "And if the worst should happen?" he asked quietly.

"Keep to the code," answered Jack. "You know that."

Chapter
16

Jack and Will rowed into the still waters of the cave, where the air was moist and thick. On the wall hung a lantern, and to one side, Will could see the skeleton of a man half buried in the sand, a sword still stuck in his back.

As they drifted past the poor blighter, Will asked Jack a question. "What code is Gibbs to keep to, if the worst should happen?"

Jack kept rowing. "Pirates' code," he said. "Any man who falls behind is left behind."

Suddenly, several small bright circles began to shimmer on the wall of the cave, then dozens more. Will looked around but couldn't find the source. Then he glanced down into the water and saw thousands of gold coins reflecting the light from the lantern: all of it treasure that had been spilled from the many trips Barbossa and his pirates had made into the cave.

Will and Jack silently rowed to a landing where the pirates had moored their longboats. Will pulled the boat ashore. Jack hopped out and led Will up a short slope.

Carefully, they looked over the top into a vast cavern. Will couldn't believe what he saw. The entire cavern was filled with the most spectacular treasure.

Glittering in the pirates' torchlight were bars of silver; gold boxes set with diamonds; rings with sparkling jewels; rubies large and small; great, long strings of pearls; brightly coloured silks; and piles of gold dust and coins. At the centre of the cave, the pirates emptied trunks of gold and silver around Elizabeth, who stood bound next to an Aztec stone chest.

Will tried to scramble over the top of the rise to save her, but Jack held him back. "We wait for the opportune moment!" he whispered.

But Will was in no mood to wait. Elizabeth's

life was at stake. "Sorry, Jack . . . but I'm not going to be your leverage," he said, and brought an oar down over Jack's head. The monkey suddenly looked up, but then swivelled his little head around when Captain Barbossa began to speak.

"You know the first thing I'm going to do after this curse is lifted?" he asked, grinning at Elizabeth. "Eat a whole bushel of apples!" The pirates laughed as Barbossa raised his knife and sliced the middle of Elizabeth's palm. He placed the medallion in her hand and closed her fist around it.

Barbossa took the bloody medallion from her and dropped it into the stone chest. "Begun by blood, by blood undone!" he shouted.

The pirates tensed, waiting to see what would happen when the curse was finally lifted. "I don't feel no different," said the one-eyed pirate after a time. The men looked at one another. "How do we tell?" Pintel asked.

Barbossa frowned, took out his pistol, and shot Pintel in the chest! The crew was completely disappointed when Pintel didn't fall down dead.

"It didn't work!" they complained. "The curse is still upon us!"

Barbossa was furious. He turned to Elizabeth and grabbed her. "You. Was your father William Turner?"

"No," gulped Elizabeth.

The pirates were in an uproar and began to shout. "You two," yelled Bo'sun, pointing at Pintel and his one-eyed friend, "you brought us the wrong person!"

"But she had the medallion, and she's the proper age!" the one-eyed pirate pleaded.

Then Bo'sun turned to Barbossa. "It's you who sent Bootstrap to the depths."

"Aye, it's you what brought us here in the first place!" yelled another. The shouting became louder, and soon every pirate was on his feet.

"I say we cut her neck and spill all her blood, just in case . . . " shouted Bo'sun.

Suddenly, Elizabeth felt a hand over her mouth. It was Will. In all the fighting, no one noticed Will untying Elizabeth. The two crouched down and headed for the water. But before they slipped away, Elizabeth grabbed the medallion.

The monkey saw it all. His screeching echoed through the cavern as he pointed towards Will and Elizabeth. Barbossa looked around and threw up his arms. "They've taken the medallion!" he yelled. "After them! Fetch it back!"

The pirates raced to their longboats, but the oars were missing! "Find 'em!" yelled Bo'sun.

Into the middle of the confusion walked Jack Sparrow, dazed from the whack on the head he'd received from Will.

"You!" said Ragetti, recognizing Jack. "You're supposed to be dead!"

"I'm not?" asked Jack, staggering around the treasure.

The pirates drew their swords and pistols and Jack came to his senses. "Parley," he said.

The pirates lowered their weapons. Pintel threw his to the ground. "Parley?" Pintel shouted. "Curses to whatever muttonhead ever thought up parley!"

Captain Barbossa stepped forward and stared at Jack. "Kill him," he said, and turned away.

Pintel happily raised his gun and was aiming

when Jack said to Barbossa, "The girl's blood didn't work, did it?"

Barbossa snapped back around. "Hold fire," he told Pintel, who was now truly disappointed.

"I know whose blood you need," Jack said.

Chapter
17

Will threw the last of the pirates' oars over the side, then helped Elizabeth board the *Interceptor*.

"Jack ain't with you?" asked Gibbs.

"Where be Jack, boy?" asked AnaMaria sternly.

Elizabeth gasped. She realized that she had been saved not only by Will – but also by the notorious pirate, Jack Sparrow.

"Fell behind," Will answered AnaMaria. Then he moved away to tend to Elizabeth. Gibbs and AnaMaria exchanged a grim glance.

"Weigh anchor and hoist the sails," AnaMaria ordered the crew, and the *Interceptor* headed out for the open sea.

Below decks, Will took out some bandages for the cut on Elizabeth's hand. As he tenderly tied the bandages around her wound, they looked into each other's eyes. Will leaned in to kiss her, but Elizabeth took his hand instead. She placed the medallion from her neck into Will's palm. "This is yours," she told him. Will looked at it, confused.

"Don't you recognize it?" she asked.

"I thought I'd lost it," answered Will. "It was a gift from my father."

Will stared at the medallion. "This is part of the treasure . . ." he said, then realized, ". . . it was *my* blood they needed. My father's blood. The blood of a pirate."

On board the *Black Pearl*, Jack roamed the cabin and examined the sorry state it was in. Captain Barbossa sat behind his desk and glowered at the man he so hated.

"I'm disappointed, Barbossa," Jack said, polishing a bit of brass with the back of his sleeve. "I expected you to take better care of my ship."

"It's not your ship," snapped Barbossa.

"The very issue we need to rectify," said Jack.

"That's the terms you're negotiating for?" asked Barbossa. "You get the *Black Pearl*? You expect to leave me standing on some beach with nothing more than a name and your word it's the one we need, and then watch you sail away on my ship?"

Jack sat down and put his feet on the desk. "Oh, no, I expect to leave you standing on some beach watching me sail away on *my* ship, and then I'll shout the name back to you!"

Jack picked up an apple and took a bite. Barbossa watched him savour the taste. "I suppose I should thank you," Jack said. "If you hadn't betrayed me and left me to die, I'd have had an equal share in the curse, same as you! Funny old world," mused Jack, enjoying his apple.

But he changed his tune when Bo'sun suddenly appeared at the cabin door. "Captain, we're coming up on the *Interceptor*," he said.

Jack quickly followed Barbossa to the deck. He worried things wouldn't go well for the *Interceptor* if it had to come up against the *Black Pearl*.

"What do you say to this?" Jack offered. "I'll go aboard and negotiate with them, get you your medallion back, and there'll be no need to swab blood off the decks later."

Barbossa shook his head. "Now, see, Jack. That's exactly the attitude that lost you the *Pearl*!

"Lock him in the brig!" he said flatly.

Barbossa took the wheel of the *Black Pearl* in his hands. "Raise the sails and run out the guns!" he shouted to his crew. "Haul on the mainsails and let go!"

The small hatches on the side of the *Black Pearl* opened, and large galley oars extended from each side of the ship. The pirates rowed in unison, and the *Black Pearl* moved faster and faster. Behind Captain Barbossa, the crew hoisted the skull and crossbones of the Jolly Roger!

On the deck of the *Interceptor*, Gibbs could see the *Black Pearl* gaining on them. "Shake out the sails!" he shouted. "I want to see every inch of canvas we've got!"

"What's happening?" Elizabeth asked when she heard the commotion on deck. Then she saw the *Black Pearl* on the horizon.

"Lighten the ship!" shouted AnaMaria in

hopes of getting the *Interceptor* to pick up some speed and outrun the *Black Pearl*. "Anything we can afford to lose, see it's lost!"

From the deck, the crew threw crates, barrels, and cannonballs over the side. But the *Black Pearl* was gaining fast. It was almost on them! "We're going to have to fight!" shouted AnaMaria. "Load the guns!"

"*Uh-oh!*" squawked Cotton's parrot. The cannonballs were already over the side, so the crew loaded everything they could find into the guns: silverware, nails, even crushed glass!

Barbossa knew the *Interceptor* would never get a shot off unless the *Black Pearl* came up alongside, so he stayed to its stern.

Elizabeth saw the problem and had an idea. "Drop the anchor!" she shouted to AnaMaria.

"You're daft!" AnaMaria shouted back, but Gibbs got the idea.

"Do it!" he yelled to the crew. "Or it's you we'll be loading into the cannons!"

The anchor splashed into the water, hit the bottom and caught on the reef. The anchor line went taut and the *Interceptor* heaved as it pivoted in a circle, bringing it broadside to the *Black Pearl*.

"Fire all!" shouted AnaMaria.

Barbossa raised his cutlass and cried out for more cannon fire. The two ships opened fire!

On the gun deck of the *Black Pearl*, Pintel looked over to see a spoon embedded in a post beside his head. Then he saw Ragetti with a fork stuck in that blasted wooden eye! He yanked on the fork and managed to pull the eye out with it. The two looked at each other and shook their heads.

Below decks, the door of the brig was blown off by a blast of cannon. "Stop putting holes in my ship!" shouted Jack as he pushed through the door. "That's it, I'm putting an end to this," he huffed, coming up on the *Black Pearl*'s deck.

Barbossa ordered a second round of fire on the *Interceptor*. The blast shattered the ship's mainmast. The mast leaned, then came crashing down across the *Black Pearl*, smashing the deck next to Barbossa.

He didn't flinch. "Find me that medallion!" he

shouted to his crew. The monkey scampered across the fallen mast, followed by a swarm of pirates swinging from the rigging.

One pirate missed his landing and swung backwards. Jack intercepted the line with a thank-you salute to the pirate as he splashed into the sea.

Jack leaped out on the line as the two crews battled on the decks below him. Then he saw Gibbs with pirates coming at him from both sides. Jack swung down and hit the first one hard, then swung back and got the second. "Jack, you're alive!" Gibbs shouted to his old friend as Jack dropped onto the main deck.

Chapter
18

Below the deck of the *Interceptor*, the blast of a cannon had knocked a beam across the door of Will's cabin. The water was rising fast, and Will couldn't get the door to budge. He was pulling with all his might when a screech turned his head. It was the cursed monkey. The monkey grabbed the medallion and made his way back out through a hole in the bulkhead.

The water was almost to the top of the cabin. Desperate, Will took a breath and went under.

On the deck, the monkey raced past Jack, who saw that the animal had the medallion. Jack chased him across the broken mast back to the *Black Pearl*. He was about to snatch the medallion from the monkey's nasty little paw when a hand reached down and grabbed it.

"Why, thank you, Jack," Barbossa said with an unpleasant grin.

"You're welcome," Jack replied grimly.

"Not you," Barbossa said. "We named the monkey Jack."

It seemed that all was lost. Barbossa's pirates had overtaken the *Interceptor*, and it was sinking fast. Gibbs finally signalled their surrender as Barbossa raised the medallion. "The prize is ours!" he shouted to his cheering pirates.

Jack's crew was roughly taken aboard the *Black Pearl* and tied to the mast by Pintel and Ragetti.

"Any of you so much as thinks the word 'parley', I'll have your guts for garters!" Pintel said, holding his pistol on them.

Suddenly, a huge explosion came from the battered *Interceptor*, the debris landing on the *Black Pearl*'s deck.

There, standing on the rail and soaking wet, was Will, alive and well and pointing a pistol at

Barbossa's head. "She goes free!" he demanded.

"What's in your head, boy? You've got one shot . . . and we can't die."

"You can't. I can," said Will, putting the gun's muzzle under his chin. "My name is Will Turner," he announced. "My father was Bootstrap Bill Turner. His blood runs in my veins!"

Every pirate on deck looked at Will in surprise, but Jack only shook his head in dismay.

"Why, it's the spittin' image of old Bootstrap, come back to haunt us!" said Ragetti.

"And on my word," said Will as he cocked the trigger, "do as I say, or I will pull the trigger and sink all the way down to Davy Jones's locker!"

"Name your terms, Mr Turner," said Barbossa flatly. He knew that if Will pulled the trigger, they'd be cursed forever.

"Elizabeth goes free!" Will answered.

"Yes, we know that one," said Barbossa. "Anything else?"

Will hadn't thought that far ahead. "And Jack," he finally added. "He goes free, too. And the crew . . . they're not to be harmed! Agree!" he demanded as he leaned out over the water.

"Agreed," Barbossa said. "You have my word as a gentleman of fortune."

"You can't trust him!" Elizabeth shouted.

"You can trust this," Barbossa hissed, grinding his teeth. "Pull that trigger and the girl will be the first to suffer – and the last to die!"

Will slowly lowered his gun. Pirates immediately swarmed him. Fearing what might happen next, Jack stepped up to Barbossa. "What about our bargain?" he demanded.

"I've got the *Pearl*, and I've got the child of Bootstrap Bill now. And you've got–" he glared hard at Jack "–nothing to bargain with.

"But no worries, Jack. See that island over there?" Barbossa asked, pointing to a patch of sea-washed sand. "If memory serves, it be the same one we made you governor of on our last trip. I'll wager that by whatever miracle you escaped before, you won't be able to conjure it again. For you or the girl!"

"You swore they'd go free!" Will protested.

"Aye, so I did . . . and so they will," agreed Barbossa. "But you never made specific mention of when, nor where."

Will struggled furiously against the pirates who now held him back.

"Men!" Barbossa shouted to his crew. "The plank!"

Chapter
19

A shark's fin glided past the *Black Pearl* as Jack, hands tied behind his back, stood on the plank. "Last time you left me a pistol with one shot," he said before taking the step that would land him in the company of the sharks below.

"By the powers, you're right!" said Barbossa, enjoying the moment. "Where's Jack's pistol?" he asked the crew. "Bring it forward!"

"Seeing that there's two of us," Jack said, nodding at Elizabeth, "a gentleman would give us two pistols."

"It'll be one pistol, as before," Barbossa answered, taking Jack's pistol from one of the pirates, "and *you* can be the gentleman, an' shoot the lady, and starve to death yourself!"

The pirates hooted with laughter as Barbossa took Jack's gun and tossed it over the side.

Jack suddenly felt the point of a cutlass at his back and stumbled off the edge of the plank. He plunged straight down into the water.

"The lady's next!" declared Barbossa.

The pirates took her by both arms. Elizabeth remained calm. She showed the pirates no fear as she stepped onto the plank. She turned once and looked back at Will. She was about to say something to him when Bo'sun shook the plank and she tumbled off the end.

Bubbles foamed around Elizabeth as she plunged into the sea. She opened her eyes underwater and saw fish scatter in all directions. Then she looked up and saw the circling sharks— hammerheads, their dark shapes gliding through the warm turquoise water.

She held her breath, turning her head and looking for Jack. She saw him swimming towards the bottom, his hands still tied behind his back. She dived down, grabbed at the ropes and untied him.

Jack immediately swam to the bottom, ran his hands through the sand, and found the pistol.

Elizabeth began to swim for the surface, but Jack grabbed her ankle and jerked her back down. She struggled, then looked at Jack, who was shaking his head, pointing up at the sharks.

Jack forced Elizabeth to swim along the bottom with him until they reached the reef. Finally, they both surfaced, choking and gasping for air.

"Why?" coughed Elizabeth, not understanding why Jack had held her under.

"Sharks attack from below," he said, breathing hard. She nodded grimly.

Jack turned and looked out to sea. The *Black Pearl* was quickly moving away under full sail. "That's the second time I've had to watch that man sail away with my ship!" he said angrily.

Jack and Elizabeth swam the little bit of sea that separated the reef from the island.

"Not all that big, is it?" commented Elizabeth when they got to shore. Jack didn't seem to be bothered by the size of the island. He'd been marooned and left to die on it before.

As Elizabeth walked the shore, Jack took apart his pistol and laid it out on his bandana. When it was dry, he reassembled it and began digging a deep hole.

"What are you doing?" Elizabeth asked him.

Jack grabbed hold of a large iron ring at the bottom of the hole and began to pull.

"Is there a boat under there?" she asked excitedly. "Is that how you escaped the last time?"

"In a way . . . " answered Jack as he heaved a trap door open, revealing a deep, dark pit. Inside, he could see barrels of rum covered with dust and cobwebs.

Elizabeth looked at the barrels. "How will this help us get away?" she asked.

"It won't," sighed Jack, jumping into the pit and opening a bottle of rum, "and so we won't."

"But you did it before!"

"Last time," explained Jack as he took a swig of the rum, "I was here for a grand total of three days. Last time, the rum-runners who used this island as a hiding place came by, and I bartered passage off. But from the looks here," he said, running his hand through the cobwebs, "they've long been taken out of business." He took another swig of rum, then added, "We probably have your friend Norrington to credit for that."

Elizabeth was shocked. "So that's it?" she asked, hoping for a better explanation. "You spent three days lying on the beach drinking rum?"

"Welcome to the Caribbean, love," sighed Jack as he gathered a few bottles and headed for the beach.

"You should look at it this way," he told her as he began to build a fire. "We've got some food on the trees. And we've got rum. We can stay alive a month, maybe more."

"A month?" exclaimed Elizabeth. "Will doesn't have a month! We have to do something now!"

"Ah, you're right," Jack answered, and raised his bottle. "Here's luck to you, Will Turner!"

Elizabeth sat down next to the fire and took a bottle of rum herself. She forced down a sip and began to sing, *"Drink up, me hearties, yo ho . . ."*

"What – what was that?" Jack asked.

"It's nothing. A song I learned about pirates when I was a child," she told him.

"I know a lot of songs about pirates, but none

I'd teach a child," Jack said, tossing Elizabeth another bottle of rum. "Let's hear it."

Elizabeth began to sing, softly at first, but then more boldly:

"We pillage, we plunder, we rifle, we loot,
Drink up, me hearties, yo ho!

We kidnap, we ravage and don't give a hoot,
Drink up, me hearties, yo ho!

Yo ho, yo ho, a pirate's life for me,
Yo ho, yo ho, a pirate's life for me…"

"I *love* this song!" exclaimed Jack, and began to sing along.

"We're beggars and blighters and ne'er-do-well
cads,
Drink up, me hearties, yo ho!

Aye, but we're loved by our mums and
our dads,
Drink up, me hearties, yo ho!"

The *Interceptor* is the fastest ship in the
Caribbean Sea and the pride of Port Royal.

Young Elizabeth Swann watches over Will Turner.

Commodore Norrington vows to rid the sea of pirates.

Elizabeth's father wants her to marry Norrington,
but she wants nothing to do with the rigid commodore.

Swashbuckler Jack Sparrow plots to get his ship, the *Black Pearl*, back from Captain Barbossa.

The evil pirate Barbossa finally finds the last piece of cursed gold.

Jack and Will Turner take possession of the *Interceptor* to save Elizabeth from Barbossa and his pirate crew.

Barbossa tells Elizabeth how he plans to lift the curse from his crew . . . with her blood!

The gold is returned – but Barbossa
and his crew are still cursed!

As a joke, the pirates name their mean little monkey Jack after Jack Sparrow.

The bumbling pirates Pintel and Ragetti never get anything right.

Free of Barbossa and his crew, Will and Jack
take command of the *Black Pearl* once more.

Elizabeth and Will watch as Norrington
gives the order to hang Jack for piracy.

Everyone watches as Jack Sparrow
makes yet another daring escape.

Elizabeth and Will finally kiss . . . and they
live happily ever after.

The two hoisted their bottles, but only Jack drank. Elizabeth pretended to.

"When I get the *Black Pearl* back, I'm going to teach it to the whole crew, and we'll sing it *all* the time," Jack promised, finishing off the bottle.

"You'll be positively the most fearsome pirates to sail the Spanish Main!" Elizabeth saluted.

"Not just the Spanish Main," Jack said dreamily, "the whole ocean . . . the whole world. Wherever we want to go, we go. That's what a ship is, you know. Not just a keel and a hull and a deck and sails. That's what a ship needs. But what a ship is . . . what the *Black Pearl* really is . . . is freedom!"

"To freedom!" said Elizabeth in a toast.

"To the *Black Pearl*!" said Jack, tapping his bottle against Elizabeth's. Jack happily took a last sip of rum, leaned back and fell asleep, dead drunk.

Jack awoke with a huge headache the next morning. He sat up slowly and rubbed his poor head. Suddenly, he was hit with a whiff of smoke.

He looked around. The whole island was on fire, and Elizabeth was busy pouring rum on the blaze.

"What are you doing?" yelled Jack, leaping to his feet. "You've burned our food, the shade . . . the rum! Why?"

Elizabeth calmly pointed to the smoke spiralling into the sky. "That signal goes up 1,000 feet . . . it can be seen for 200 leagues in every direction. The entire Royal Navy is out looking for me . . . . Do you think there's even a chance they could miss it?" she asked Jack, who was now furious.

"You . . . you burned up the island for a one-time chance of being saved?" he asked in disbelief.

"Exactly," she said.

Jack threw his hands up and stalked off in a huff. He climbed to the top of a dune and looked out to sea. He stared for a moment, shaking his head. Then, suddenly, on the horizon, he saw white sails. *Can't be!* he thought. But sure enough, it was. The *Dauntless* was heading towards the island. They'd seen the signal and were on their way to rescue Elizabeth.

"There'll be no living with her after this!" Jack grumbled to himself.

Chapter
20

Once again, Jack found himself on the deck of the *Dauntless*, and once again, Norrington was about to throw him in the brig.

But Elizabeth was still determined to save Will, and she knew she needed Jack to do it.

A number of sailors had gathered around Jack and were ready to clap him into irons when she said, "Commodore, we must set out immediately for Isla de la Muerta! Captain Sparrow can chart the course, but he won't from the brig."

Jack nodded in agreement. "Think about it," he said to Norrington. "The *Black Pearl* . . . Barbossa . . . the last real pirate threat in the Caribbean. How can you pass that up?"

Elizabeth could see that Commodore Norrington was not convinced, nor was her father. "We are returning to Port Royal, not gallivanting after pirates," Governor Swann told her.

"Then we're condemning Will to his death," she said, and turned to Norrington. "Commodore, I beg you. Please do this . . . for me . . . as a wedding gift."

Norrington was shocked. "Am I to understand that you will accept my proposal of marriage on the condition I rescue Mr Turner?" he asked.

"Not a condition," answered Elizabeth. "I will marry you."

Jack too was shocked!

"Mr Gillette," Commodore Norrington shouted to his first mate, "take Mr Sparrow to the bridge. He'll give you the heading."

Jack stood at the helm of the *Dauntless* and set it on course for Isla de la Muerta. He knew he had to hurry. He was in a race to get to the island before Will Turner's blood could finally turn Barbossa and his cursed crew into real men.

At the same moment, aboard the *Black Pearl*, Captain Barbossa appeared with Pintel and his one-eyed friend in front of Will's cell. "Bring him," he ordered.

Jack's crew was left in their cell as the pirates piled into a longboat. They rowed with Will at gunpoint through the fog and disappeared into the mouth of the cave.

Chapter
21

Commodore Norrington lowered his spyglass. The decks of the *Black Pearl* were empty. "I don't care for the situation," he said to Jack. "Any attempt to storm the island could turn into an ambush."

"Not if you do the ambushing," Jack answered. "I'll go in and convince Barbossa to send his men out . . . leaving you to do nothing but stand on the deck of the *Dauntless* and holler, 'Fire cannons'! What do you have to lose?" asked Jack, leaving out the minor detail of the curse that made Barbossa's crew immortal.

Norrington reluctantly agreed and allowed Jack to take a longboat to the island alone.

But watching Jack smile as he rowed away, he reconsidered. "Mr Gillette, break out the longboats."

Below decks, Governor Swann was knocking on Elizabeth's cabin door, but there was no answer. Elizabeth was standing before the open stern window. She had tied her bedsheets together and was lowering herself down to a rowing boat tied alongside the *Dauntless*. The governor knocked again. "Elizabeth!" he said, but she was gone. In the light of the full moon, she was rowing the small boat towards the *Black Pearl*.

Chapter
22

Inside the cave, lit by torches and shafts of moonlight, the pirates climbed over rocks and waded through water, pushing Will along.

"No reason to fret," Pintel told Will. "It's just the prick of a finger and a few drops of blood."

But another pirate was quick to correct him. "No mistakes this time," he said, looking at Will. "He's only half Turner. We spill it all!"

Pintel shrugged. "I guess there is a reason to fret." He giggled.

Will was shoved to his knees next to the Aztec stone chest at the centre of the cavern. A pirate pushed Will's head forward so that his neck was directly over the chest. Then Barbossa put a blade to his throat.

"Excuse me," came a voice. "Pardon me. Beg pardon."

Barbossa froze in anger. *Jack Sparrow!* He was making his way through the crowd of pirates. "Not possible," said Barbossa, gritting his teeth and staring at him.

"Not probable," said Jack, knowing anything was possible.

"Jack!" shouted Will, raising his head. But a pirate pushed it back down.

Barbossa pointed his knife at Jack. "You're next!" he said as he put the knife back to Will's throat.

"You don't want to be doing that," Jack said calmly.

Barbossa clenched his fists, not wanting to ask but knowing he had to. "*Why* don't I want to do this?"

"Because the HMS *Dauntless*, pride of the Royal Navy, is floating right offshore waiting for you," answered Jack. Barbossa took the knife from

Will's throat and turned toward Jack.

Jack pointed out that if the curse was lifted, Barbossa and his crew would become living men again . . . the kind Commodore Norrington and the Royal Navy would have no trouble killing. But if they rowed out to the *Dauntless* as the cursed men they were, they could have the *Dauntless* along with the *Pearl*!

"And there you are," said Jack, "with two ships! The makings of your very own fleet," he added. Jack now had Barbossa's full attention.

"Of course, you'll take the grandest as your flagship . . . and who's to argue?" smiled Jack as he strolled over to the chest and ran his fingers through the gold coins. "But what of the *Pearl*?" he pondered out loud. The question hung in the air as Barbossa stared at him.

"Make me captain," Jack suddenly offered. "I sail under your colours. I give you ten per cent of my plunder, and you get to introduce yourself at tea parties as Commodore Barbossa."

Barbossa set his jaw. "Fifty per cent," he answered.

"Fifteen," countered Jack.

"Forty," said Barbossa.

"Twenty-five," replied Jack. "And I'll buy you the hat."

Barbossa smiled. "We have an accord," he said, and the two shook hands.

Barbossa turned his attention from Will. He'd be saving the boy's blood for later, when Norrington and his men would be dead and safely out of the way. He glared triumphantly at his crew.

"Take a walk," he told them.

Chapter
23

Outside the cave, on the still, moonlit water, Commodore Norrington and an armed crew waited in seven longboats. They were planning a surprise attack on the pirates as they emerged from the cave.

The sailors never noticed the slight ripple that moved across the water. The pirates were moving out of the cave, all right, but they did not come out in longboats. They were walking across the sea bed!

Fish scattered in every direction as the shadowy figures, weapons in hands, trudged through the shifting current. Water-filtered moonlight made them an eerie army of marching skeletons. They silently walked under Norrington's longboats and headed for the *Dauntless* unseen.

The silence was broken by a sudden splash of water. Every sailor raised his pistol as a rowing boat slowly emerged from the mouth of the cave. Norrington looked at the two figures in the boat and ordered his men to hold their fire. He couldn't believe what he was seeing. Two women were rowing the boat!

On the deck of the *Dauntless*, Gillette was keeping watch with a spyglass. He saw the two women rowing from the cave. Then he saw one of them lower her parasol in the moonlight. They were two skeletons in women's dresses, and one of them had a wooden eye!

Realizing they'd been found out, one of the skeletons raised a pistol and shot the hat off the first mate's head. Gillette gasped as the skeleton pirates who had silently boarded the ship now dropped down from the rigging like spiders. The attack on the *Dauntless* had begun!

The sound of guns alerted Norrington to the fight on the *Dauntless*. He looked back and saw the ghostly skeletons running riot over the ship. He quickly ordered his men to row back to the *Dauntless*, but a sudden round of cannon fire blew one of the longboats to pieces. Norrington was now being fired upon by the cannons of his own ship!

The sailors rowed against the barrage of cannon with all their might, firing at the pirates on the *Dauntless* as they went. Finally, Norrington's boats pulled up alongside the ship. He and his men climbed up the side. They scrambled over the rails and joined the battle raging on deck.

Norrington suddenly found himself facing a huge pirate swinging an axe at his neck. He was battling the man back and over the side when Governor Swann grabbed him. "Elizabeth!" he exclaimed in a panic. "She's gone!"

Chapter
24

Elizabeth had reached the *Black Pearl*. Desperate to save Will, she silently began to climb up the side of the ship. Then she heard voices coming from the galley. Two pirates were busy preparing a grand feast of cakes, biscuits, rum and jerky. They were waiting for Barbossa and his crew to return to the *Black Pearl* with the good news that the curse was lifted and they would finally be able to taste real food as real men!

"Which would you eat first?" asked one pirate, eyeing the feast that was laid out on the table.

"Mmm, the cake!" answered the other.

"Aye, the cake!" they agreed as Elizabeth climbed past the porthole. The ship creaked as she climbed over the gunwale and sneaked along the deck. Suddenly, out of the darkness, the monkey dropped down in front of her and shrieked. Elizabeth grabbed him by the fur with her hands and tossed him over the side. Screeching as he fell, the monkey hit the water with a splash. The two pirates looked out the porthole and down into the water . . . then up to the deck.

Elizabeth ran, but she knew the pirates had seen her. She hid in a dark corner as they charged onto the deck. Suddenly, the two pirates heard the ropes in the sails move. Turning to see where the noise was coming from, they were struck in the chest by the boom of the ship. They flew overboard, where they joined the flailing monkey.

To Elizabeth's surprise, Jack's crew stepped out of the shadows. AnaMaria and Gibbs had swung the boom, sending the last two pirates into the sea below. The *Black Pearl* was theirs!

"All of you!" Elizabeth said, relieved to see them. "Will is in that cave, and as long as we have a chance to save him, we must act! And Jack, too!" she added, trying to lower a boat into the water.

But no one raised a hand to help her. Elizabeth looked at them, confused.

"Jack owes us a ship," said AnaMaria sternly.

"And we've got the *Pearl* . . ." added Gibbs. "And then there's the code to consider."

"The code?" asked Elizabeth in disbelief. "Falls behind, left behind . . ." she muttered. "You're pirates! Hang the code!"

But the crew was sticking by it, and Elizabeth rowed out to Isla de la Muerta alone.

Inside the cave, not knowing that his beloved ship was now sailing away, Jack examined the exquisite pirate treasure more carefully.

"You're a hard man to predict," Barbossa said, watching Jack hold up a gold-and-diamond necklace.

"Me?" Jack exclaimed as he shook his head. "I'm dishonest. A dishonest man can always be trusted to be dishonest," he explained. Then, as if to illustrate the point, Jack suddenly flipped a beautiful sword off the floor into Will's hands.

"Dang it, Jack!" howled Barbossa, who knew he was in for a fight. "I was almost liking you."

Jack grabbed a sword for himself and charged at Barbossa. The two squared off, sliding over the glittering gold coins that covered the cave's floor.

Another pirate slashed at Will, who managed to turn so the pirate's sword cut the ropes from his hands. With both hands free, Will took on three pirates at once.

The sound of clashing metal echoed through the cave as Jack and Barbossa fought furiously. Then Barbossa stepped back and began to laugh. He dropped his sword and grabbed Jack's blade with both hands. "You can't beat me, Jack." He laughed, then twisted the sword from Jack's grip and drove it into Jack's chest!

Will froze. Jack looked down at the sword jutting from his ribs and staggered back into the moonlight.

"Well, isn't that interesting," remarked Jack as his own body turned into a skeleton. "That curse seemed to be so useful," he said, taking a gold coin from his pocket, "I decided to get one for myself!"

Barbossa grabbed his sword as Jack pulled his own from his chest, and the two skeletons lunged and battled in the moonlight.

"So what now, Jack Sparrow?" asked Barbossa as they duelled over chests of gold, skull to skull. "Are we to be two immortals locked in battle until Judgment Day?"

"Or you could surrender," Jack suggested. But Barbossa wasn't interested, and fiercely continued his attack.

Will was trying to fight his way out of a corner when an explosion blinded him for a moment. Two pirates pounced and were about to make short work of him when one of them was suddenly gaffed in the back!

Will slashed at the other pirate and scrambled free to find Elizabeth holding the gaff. Back to back, they fought off the pirates together.

Frustrated beyond measure, Barbossa slashed at Jack and drove him backwards toward Elizabeth.

"I swear, Sparrow," he vowed, "when my men return, I will carve and joint your body and decorate the *Black Pearl* with the pieces!" Then he reached out and grabbed Elizabeth, putting his sword to her throat.

Jack stepped back, took out his pistol, and fired the one shot he'd been saving all those years.

Barbossa looked down at the hole in his shirt and back up at Jack.

"Ten years you carry that pistol and now you waste your shot?" the pirate captain asked him.

"He didn't waste it!" Will said triumphantly, standing over the chest of Aztec gold. He slashed his palm with his knife and wrapped his hand around the gold medallion. Then he dropped the bloody medallion into the chest.

Barbossa looked down at his chest as he began to bleed from the bullet hole. The pirate gave Jack a final snarl.

Jack tossed the pistol away and Barbossa fell to the floor, dead.

At that same moment, aboard the *Dauntless*, a pirate suddenly cried out and fell to the deck. Two more stepped into the moonlight and realized they were no longer skeletons. The curse was lifted, but it was too soon for Barbossa's men.

All around the ship, pirates fell quickly to Norrington's men, and those who did not surrendered.

"Parley?" asked Pintel hopefully as he and Ragetti were led to the brig.

In the meantime, Jack had some unfinished business inside the cave of Isla de la Muerta. Using his knife, he cut his arm, then wiped the blood from the blade onto the gold coin. He held the coin over the chest but couldn't quite bring himself to drop it.

"The immortal Captain Jack Sparrow," he said dreamily. "It has a ring."

"Oh, well," he sighed, thinking better of the idea, and he dropped the coin into the chest. He then gathered some large gold pieces from the cave and happily climbed into a longboat with Will and Elizabeth. "If I could trouble you to drop me at the *Black Pearl* . . ."

But when they reached the mouth of the cave, Jack stood up in the longboat and saw that the *Black Pearl* was gone. He scanned the water, but it was no good.

"I'm sorry," Will told him as Jack sat back down.

Jack knew what his crew had done, but he bore them no grudge. "They did what's right by them," he said, knowing he would soon be on his way to meet the hangman in Fort Charles.

Chapter
25

Jack's luck finally seemed to have failed him as he stood on the wooden gallows, the hangman's noose around his neck.

Elizabeth and her father, along with Commodore Norrington, were in the crowd for the proceedings. "This is wrong," Elizabeth pleaded. "He risked his life to rescue me, and then risked it again to save your crew." But in her father's eyes, the law was the law, and in the Crown's eyes, Jack had broken it.

Will was also on hand, moving through the crowd that had come to see the pirate hang. As the drums began to roll and the executioner moved his hand towards the lever, Will noticed a green bird landing on a ledge. It was Cotton's parrot! It looked directly at Will –

it was a signal – and Will gave Jack a nod.

Will stepped up to Elizabeth and drew his sword. "I love you," he told her. "I should have told you a long time ago."

Before she could say a word, Will dashed to the gallows, drawing a second sword as the executioner pulled the lever. Will leaped to the stairs of the gallows and buried his sword in the top of the trap door. It opened and Jack fell. But the sword stuck sideways from the trap door, and Jack's feet found it before he was hanged.

Jack balanced on the blade. Will swung his sword and severed the hangman's rope, freeing Jack, who pulled the sword from the trap door as he fell; then he hit the ground, brandishing the weapon.

Jack and Will battled Norrington's guards under the gallows until they reached the parapet of the fort. But with the sea at their backs, they had nowhere left to go. The troops raised their rifles. Jack and Will were cornered.

Suddenly, Will stepped up and put himself between Jack and the armed guards. They'd have to shoot him before they could get to Jack.

Governor Swann pushed to the front with Norrington. "I granted you clemency and this is how you repay me?" he demanded of Will. "You throw in with *him*? He is a pirate!"

"And a good man!" Will shouted to Norrington.

"You forget your place, Turner," said the commodore.

"It's right here, between you and Jack," Will replied.

Elizabeth pushed her way through the crowd and jumped onto the parapet next to Will. "As is mine!" she declared.

"This is where your heart truly lies, then?" Norrington asked Elizabeth.

"It is," Elizabeth said.

Jack, Will and Elizabeth stared at Norrington. For a moment his eyes glinted with fierce determination. Then they could all see his face soften as he looked at Elizabeth. It was obvious that he realized the folly of their showdown. She would never love him the way she loved Will.

"I was rooting for you, mate," Jack said, giving Norrington a nod of condolence. Then he turned to the crowd and shouted, "Friends, this is the day you will always remember as the day you *almost* hung . . ." But before he could finish, Jack slipped off the parapet and tumbled into the sea below.

The crowd hurried to the stone wall. Jack could be seen swimming through the water. Sailing into the harbour, the crowd also saw the *Black Pearl*. Standing on her deck was Jack's crew, come back to save their captain!

Turning to Will, Norrington said, "This is a very nice sword. I expect the man who made it to show the same care and devotion to all aspects of his life." He saluted Will with the sword and added, "My compliments."

He then turned to Elizabeth and said cheerfully, "Miss Swann. The best of luck to you both."

Gillette raced up to the commodore and asked if he should prepare the *Dauntless* to pursue Jack.

"I think we can afford him one day's head start," Norrington replied with a smile. "More sporting that way."

On the parapet, Will and Elizabeth gazed into each other's eyes for a long moment. Then Will swept her up into his arms and kissed her.

"But he's a blacksmith," grieved the poor governor.

"No," said Elizabeth proudly. "He's a pirate!"

Chapter
26

From the fantail of the *Black Pearl*, Cotton, with his parrot on his shoulder, threw a line to Jack.

Jack grabbed the line as it swept by, and climbed to the deck of the *Black Pearl*. Gibbs greeted him with a salute.

"I thought I told you to keep to the code," Jack said to him seriously.

Gibbs shuffled his feet. "They're more what you might call guidelines . . ." he offered. Jack smiled. He continued up to the bow, where AnaMaria was standing at the wheel. She stepped away and said, "Captain Sparrow . . . the *Black Pearl* is yours."

Jack lovingly ran his hand along the rail, then took the wheel of the ship – his ship. He opened his compass and set his course. Satisfied with himself, he looked out to sea and began to sing himself a tune.

"*Yo ho, yo ho, a pirate's life for me . . .*"

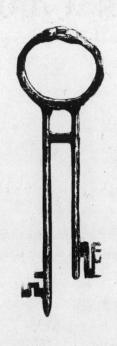

DISNEP

PIRATES of the CARIBBEAN
DEAD MAN'S CHEST

Adapted by Irene Trimble

Based on the screenplay written by
Ted Elliott and Terry Rossio
Based on characters created by Ted Elliott and Terry Rossio
and Stuart Beattie and Jay Wolpert
Based on Walt Disney's *Pirates of the Caribbean*
Produced by Jerry Bruckheimer
Directed by Gore Verbinski

Chapter 1

The moon rose high above a dark ocean. The quiet sounds of the sea – blowing wind, lapping waves and creaking lines – filled the night with an eerie symphony. On the walls of a stone prison that overlooked the scene, a flock of crows alighted. The moonlit night was made even eerier by the grunts, moans and rattling chains of captive prisoners.

A pair of guards dragged a prisoner in through the tower's stone doorway. The passage was clearly the way *into* the prison. The way *out* was very different indeed, as a number of unfortunate captives were about to learn.

More guards, carrying six wooden coffins, made their way to a wall on the prison's seaward side. With a quick condemnation, they shoved each of the coffins off the wall, allowing them to plummet down and splash into the hungry sea below. The coffins bobbed to the surface, and the tide began to carry them out like a fleet of haunted vessels. Two of the pine boxes sailed lower than the rest and began to sink slowly into the black sea.

One of the crows flew down from the prison wall, landing on a coffin. *Peck-peck, peck-peck.* He began to tap away at the wood. *Peck-peck-PECK.* The repetitive *peck-PECK-peck-PECK* was just another sound to fill the shadowy night. *Peck-PECK-peck.* It was also extremely annoying.

The person inside the coffin that the bird had chosen agreed. *Peck-peck-peck-PECK.* Suddenly, a gunshot was fired from inside the coffin that sent the bird blasting off in a cloud of feathers. An arm reached through the newly formed hole, found the latch that held the coffin closed and swung the lid open. Captain Jack Sparrow, the wiliest pirate ever to sail the high seas, quickly emerged and looked around. He was wearing his usual getup – well-worn clothing, knee-high boots and his signature red bandana. His gold tooth gleamed in the moonlight.

Jack didn't seem concerned with his situation – at first. Then his eyes grew wide and he began frantically searching the coffin. After a moment filled with high anxiety, he finally found what he thought he might have lost – his hat! With it placed firmly on his head at a smart angle, Jack was once again relaxed.

He bowed his head, crossed himself and reached down into the coffin one more time. "Sorry, mate," he said as he pulled and tugged until – SNAP – he plucked off the leg bone of his coffin mate. "Necessity is a mother," he noted with a grin. He used the bone for an oar and rowed toward the moonlit hull of his ship, the *Black Pearl*. She was patiently waiting for him out in the still water, covered by the dark of night.

Gibbs, an old salt and a fine pirate, was waiting on the *Pearl*'s deck for Jack's return. "Not quite according to plan?" Gibbs questioned, staring at Jack, who sat rowing a coffin with a leg bone in his hands. Gibbs helped his captain aboard.

"Complications arose," Jack said, tossing the leg bone overboard. "But I've found if you ask right, there's always someone willing to give a leg up."

Gibbs looked over the side of the ship at the one-legged skeleton. "Not in my experience,"

Gibbs said, shaking his head. "Can't go wrong expecting the worst from people."

Jack sighed. "It probably does save time," he said as he walked away from Gibbs. As he moved along the boat, Jack took a rolled piece of cloth from his sleeve. He began to examine it very carefully.

"Is that what you went in to find?" a toothless pirate named Leech asked anxiously. Every man on board was hungry for news of what treasure Jack had found.

"Aye, but I haven't had time to properly assess the prize," Jack answered with a sly smile. He did not seem willing to share just yet.

Suddenly, a small monkey swung out of the ship's rigging, landed in front of Jack and screeched as if he were the devil himself. Jack screamed back as the monkey snatched the roll of cloth and took it up into the sails.

Each time the monkey passed through a shaft of moonlight, it turned into a skeleton from head to tail – the result of a curse that had not been lifted. The monkey was the living dead. The horrible little beast's previous owner was the cursed Captain Barbossa, who had mutinied against Jack. Barbossa had named the monkey Jack, as a way to add insult to injury.

Jack hated the creature. He drew his pistol and aimed at the cursed monkey. Jack fired, but the gun only clicked. His shot had already been used on that blasted pecking crow. Jack grabbed a pistol from the belt of another pirate and fired again.

This time he hit his mark. The monkey was blown back and the cloth dropped from its grasp. But the monkey quickly jumped back up again, grinning.

Gibbs gave Jack a look. "You know that doesn't do any good," he told him, pointing to the gun.

Jack shrugged. "Keeps my aim sharp," he said as one of the pirates on deck scrambled to catch the falling piece of cloth. The monkey continued to screech.

"Why'd that eviscerated simian have to be the only thing to survive *Isla de Muerta*?" Jack grumbled. Then he saw the pirate who had caught the cloth examining it.

"It's a key," the pirate said, cocking his head to the side and squinting an eye.

"Even better," Jack added, raising a finger. "It's a *drawing* of a key."

The confused crew looked to Gibbs for an explanation.

"Captain," Gibbs said, clearing his throat, "I think we were expecting something a bit more . . . rewarding. What with *Isla de Muerta* going all pear shaped, reclaimed by the sea and all . . ."

"Unfortunate turn of circumstance," Jack agreed, remembering the island where the crew had had its most recent adventure, where Jack had finally defeated Barbossa *and* where he had reclaimed the *Black Pearl*.

". . . and then spending months fighting to get the British navy off our stern," Gibbs reminded him.

"Inevitable outcome of *le vie de boucanier*," Jack replied with a wave of his hand.

"We've been losing crew at every port, and it seems to us what's left that it's been a stretch since we've done even a speck of honest pirating," Gibbs continued.

Jack turned to his crew. "Is that how you're feeling?" he asked. "That I'm not serving your interests as captain?"

The crew shifted uncomfortably and then

suddenly a parrot squawked the only reply.

"ABANDON SHIP!"

The parrot belonged to the mute pirate Cotton and it spoke for him.

Jack drew his pistol again. "What did the bird say?"

"Cotton's parrot don't speak for the lot of us," Leech told Jack quickly. "*We* think you're doing a fine job."

"ABANDON SHIP," the parrot called out even louder. Jack was about to shoot the old bird, but lowered his gun instead. Cotton seemed relieved.

"At least there's one honest . . . man amongst you," Jack said, looking at Cotton's parrot. Jack shook his head and got down to the business at hand. He had questions to answer.

"Gentlemen, what do keys do?" Jack asked.

The anxious crew of rogues looked at each other. "They unlock things?" Leech asked, suddenly excited.

Jack made a face as if to say, "Yes, and . . ."

"And whatever this unlocks, inside is something valuable," Gibbs added, imagining chests of gold. "So, we're setting out to find whatever this unlocks!"

Jack shook his head. "No. If we don't have the key, we can't open whatever it unlocks, so what purpose would be served in finding whatever needs be unlocked without first having found the key that unlocks it? Honestly. Ninny."

The rowdy crew was very confused. They tried to follow along as best they could. "So, we're going to find this key?" Gibbs asked.

Jack looked into the crew members' blank faces and sighed. "What good is a key if we have nothing for the key to unlock? Please," Jack pleaded, "try and keep up!"

"So, do we have a heading?" another pirate asked.

"Aye! A heading!" Jack said. He turned away, took out his Compass and flipped it open. It was the very same Compass that had led him to *Isla de Muerta* and the caves of hidden treasure. But the readings on the Compass seemed to make Jack a bit uneasy now.

He snapped the Compass shut and waved his arm. "Set sail in a general . . . that way direction," he finally said, waving his hand dismissively out towards the sea.

"Captain?" Gibbs asked, confused. This was not typical Captain Jack Sparrow behaviour.

"I'll plot our course later. Now snap to and make sail!" he ordered as he marched off to his cabin. The crew stood and watched silently. "You know how it works!" Jack shouted impatiently and slammed his cabin door.

The crew unhappily began to get ready to sail. "Have you noticed lately, the captain seems to be acting a bit . . . strange?" a pirate whispered to Gibbs.

"Aye," Gibbs answered. "Something's got him setting a course without knowing his own heading. And I thought there was neither man nor beast alive could make him do that."

Chapter 2

While Jack's crew dealt with their captain's stranger-than-usual behaviour, a couple who should have been celebrating the happiest day of their lives was trying to avert disaster – a ruined wedding.

Outside a small seaside chapel in the Caribbean town of Port Royal, palm trees bent in the wind as rain drenched all the preparations for the nuptial celebration to be held that day. The bride, Elizabeth Swann, kneeled in her rain-soaked wedding dress, tears mixing with rain. Around her was an empty altar, overturned chairs . . . and no groom. Slowly, the young woman rose and entered the chapel to wait, her head in her hands.

The approaching sound of chains made Elizabeth look up. Through her tears she saw a man in uniform enter the chapel. He was followed by a company of marines who were dragging a prisoner. To her shock, it was her groom, Will Turner.

"Will!" Elizabeth called out. "What is happening?"

Will struggled toward her. "I don't know," he said sadly, taking in Elizabeth's ruined white satin dress.

Will had been taken prisoner earlier when marines battered down the door of his blacksmith shop and put him in irons. It didn't look like he'd be married today, after all. But waiting for his future wife, Elizabeth, was something Will was used to. He had loved her since Elizabeth and her father, the Governor of Port Royal, found Will drifting on the sea when he was ten years old. For years he had waited patiently, hoping she would finally love him back. And then she had. But it seemed that once again they would be kept apart.

Even now, standing there in chains, he couldn't help getting sentimental. "You look beautiful," Will said softly.

Elizabeth smiled. "You know it's bad luck for the groom to see the bride before the wedding."

"That explains the unexpected guests," he said, nodding at the company of red-coated marines surrounding them.

Their tender moment was interrupted by an authoritative voice. It was Elizabeth's father.

"You! Order your men to stand down and remove these shackles at once," the governor commanded.

The man in charge of the arrest made no move. "Governor Wetherby Swann," he answered. "My apologies for arriving without an invitation."

Governor Swann studied the man's face for a moment. "Cutler Beckett?" he finally asked.

"It's *Lord*, now, actually," Beckett replied.

"Lord or not, you have no reason and no authority to arrest this man."

"In fact, I do. Mr Mercer?" he said to an undistinguished-looking gentleman standing off to the side. Mercer opened a large dispatch case and handed Beckett several documents.

Beckett ceremoniously read off his newly appointed powers by the Royal Commission for Antilles Trade and Protection, then produced a warrant for the arrest of one William Turner.

Governor Swann looked at the warrant. But it wasn't for Will. "This is for Elizabeth Swann!" he exclaimed.

"Is it?" Beckett asked. "How odd . . . my mistake. Arrest her," he suddenly ordered.

The soldiers grabbed Elizabeth. "On what charges?" Elizabeth demanded.

Beckett ignored her as he shuffled through his papers. "Aha," he said, holding up another document. "Here's the warrant for William Turner. And I have another one for a James Norrington. Any idea where he is?"

"Commodore Norrington resigned his commission several months ago," Governor Swann answered quickly, "and we haven't seen him since."

Elizabeth gritted her teeth. She had once been betrothed to Norrington, though she never loved him. She suddenly found herself thinking about all she and Will – and Jack Sparrow – had been through.

Elizabeth was kidnapped by Barbossa and his men. To rescue her from the cursed pirate, Will had broken Jack Sparrow out of jail, only to be captured himself. In desperation, Elizabeth had agreed to marry Norrington in exchange for his help in saving Will. When the adventure had ended, Norrington had grudgingly agreed to give Jack Sparrow a day's head start before he would begin chasing him. It was only fair, as the pirate had saved Elizabeth. But even though it was the fair thing to do, Norrington had never forgiven himself for letting Sparrow slip away. He had lost his post and disappeared from Port Royal, disgraced.

"We are British subjects under jurisdiction of the King's Governor of Port Royal, and we demand to know the charges against us," Elizabeth said bravely, coming back to the present.

Beckett looked at his prisoners. When he finally spoke up, he sounded more than happy to make his announcement. "The charge is conspiring to secure the unlawful release of a convict condemned to death. For which, regrettably, the punishment is also death. You do remember a pirate named, I believe it is, Jack Sparrow?"

Will and Elizabeth exchanged a look. "*Captain* Jack Sparrow," they said in unison.

"Yes. I thought you might," Beckett answered, satisfied. He motioned to his men to haul the prisoners away.

Chapter 3

While Will and Elizabeth tried to sort out their current mess, Captain Jack Sparrow was dealing with problems of his own. Alone in his cabin aboard the *Black Pearl*, Jack held his Compass tightly in his hand. He sneaked a look at it once, snapped it shut, shook it and looked again. *Still* not to his liking. Jack reached for a bottle of rum. As the tattered cuff of his sleeve fell back, the branded letter *P* showed on his wrist.

Jack raised the bottle and sighed. It was empty. "Why is the rum always gone?" he asked himself. He lurched towards the cabin door and onto the main deck in search of another bottle.

"Heading, Captain?" Leech asked as Jack staggered past the wheel.

"Steady as she goes," Jack ordered, stumbling toward the ship's hold.

Below deck, pirates snored loudly as they

slept in their hammocks. A cage of chickens clucked as Jack entered. The captain raised his pistol and the chickens suddenly went quiet.

"That's what I thought," Jack said. Then he continued on.

Steadying himself on the ship's timbers, Jack made his way to the rum locker. He raised an eyebrow as he checked the racks. All were nearly empty.

Happily, Jack spied a bottle on a lower shelf and tugged it free. The bottle was encrusted with barnacles. Something was wrong. Jack uncorked it, looked inside and turned it over. Sand spilled out onto the deck.

"Time's run out, Jack," a voice suddenly said from the shadows. Jack turned. The face he saw was covered with starfish and barnacles. Crabs crawled up the man's arm as he stepped toward Jack.

"Bootstrap?" Jack asked, barely recognizing the voice. "Bill Turner?"

"Aye, Jack Sparrow. You look good."

Jack looked at the gruesome sailor. He wished he could say the same for him. He actually tried a few times, but couldn't bring himself to say it.

"Is this a dream?" Jack asked instead.

"No," Bootstrap Bill Turner, Will's father, answered flatly.

Jack shrugged. "I thought not. If it were, there'd be rum."

Bootstrap grinned and offered Jack a bottle. Jack pried the bottle from Bill's hand, uncorked it and sniffed it to be sure. Rum it was. Jack wiped the mouth of the bottle with his sleeve and took a long drink.

Bootstrap watched. "You got the *Pearl* back, I see." But Jack couldn't focus on his old shipmate's words. He was staring at the slithering, sliding sea life that lived on the man's skin.

The captain snapped himself out of it. "I had some help retrieving the *Pearl*. Your son," he said.

Bootstrap looked surprised. "William? He ended up a pirate, after all?"

Jack nodded, then added, "He's got an unhealthy streak of honesty to him."

"That's something, then," Bill told him. "Though no credit to me." The crustacean-crusted pirate fell silent.

"And to what do I owe the pleasure of your carbuncle?" Jack finally asked.

"Davy Jones," Bootstrap answered. "He sent me as an emissary."

Jack had been expecting this. "Ah, he shanghaied you into service, then."

"I chose it. I'm sorry for the part I played in mutinying against you," Bootstrap said sincerely. Jack waved it off and took another swig of rum. Bootstrap had been part of the *Black Pearl*'s crew when Barbossa mutinied. All the rest of the crew had decided to follow Barbossa and make him their captain. Jack had been left on an island to die.

"Everything went wrong after that," Bootstrap told him. "I ended up cursed, doomed to the depths of the ocean, unable to move, unable to die."

Jack shuddered.

"All I could do was think," Bootstrap continued. "And mostly I thought if I had even the tiniest hope of escaping this fate, I would take it. Trade anything for it."

"That is the kind of thinking bound to catch *his* attention," Jack said, knowing more than a bit about Jones's love for a good bargain.

"It did," Bootstrap said, nodding with regret.

"Davy Jones came. Made the offer. I could spend one hundred years before his mast, with the hope that after, I would go on to a peaceful rest."

Bootstrap stopped talking and looked his former captain in the eye. Then he added, "You made a deal with him, too, Jack. He raised the *Pearl* from the depths for you, and 13 years you've been her captain."

"Technically . . ." Jack said, about to object, but Bootstrap stopped him.

"You won't be able to talk your way out of this," Bootstrap warned as a crab crawled down his arm. The cursed pirate crushed it and shoved it into his mouth. "The terms what applied to me apply to you as well. One soul, bound to crew a lifetime aboard his ship."

But Jack wasn't about to let himself start looking like old Bootstrap any time soon. "The *Flying Dutchman* already has a captain," Jack argued, pointing out that Jones was the captain of the ghostly ship. "So there's no need of me."

Bootstrap expected as much from Jack. Captain Jack Sparrow never went down without a fight. Bootstrap sighed and nodded. "Then it's the locker for you, Jack. Jones's leviathan will find you and drag the *Pearl* back to the depths . . . and you along with it."

"Any idea when Jones will release said terrible beastie?" Jack asked, trying not to sound too worried.

Bootstrap raised an arm and pointed to Jack's hand. Jack took a step back, but it was too late. On his palm appeared the dreaded Black Spot. Jack stared at it. He was now a marked man.

"It's not a matter of how long till it comes after you," Bootstrap said as Jack looked down at the spot. "It's a matter of how long till you're found."

Jack looked up and Bootstrap Bill was gone. Jack let out a yelp and ran.

"On deck!" he yelled to his sleeping crew as he passed through the hold. "All hands! Lift the skin up. Scurry! Movement, I want movement!"

As the groggy pirates dragged themselves to their stations, Jack looked into the *Pearl*'s black sails. "Haul those sheets!" he ordered the men. "Haul 'em! Run, mates, run, as if the devil himself is on us!"

While the crew was distracted, Jack wrapped his hand in a rag to cover the Black Spot. He couldn't let anyone see that he was marked.

Gibbs looked for Jack and found him hiding behind the mast.

"Do we have a heading?" he asked.

"Land!" Jack yelled back.

"What port?" Gibbs asked.

"I said land! Any land!" Just then Jack the monkey jumped from the rigging, landed on Jack's shoulder and knocked the captain's hat overboard.

"Jack's hat!" Gibbs cried, knowing how fond of it the captain was. "Bring the ship about!"

"No!" Jack snapped. "Leave it."

Jack's crew stood stunned. They knew how much the hat meant to him. They could not believe he would actually *not* want to retrieve it. "Mind your stations, the lot of you!" Gibbs ordered, and then he turned to Jack. "For the love of mother and child, Jack, what's coming after us?"

Chapter 4

Captain Jack Sparrow's legendary three-cornered hat floated on the tide, turning slowly. By next morning, it had drifted far from the *Black Pearl*.

The hull of a small fishing vessel passed it and suddenly the hat was snatched up by a boat hook. A short, round sailor pulled it from the water and was pleased with the look of the hat. He quickly tried it on.

Just then, his mate yanked it off his head. The two were pulling on the hat when a shudder suddenly ran through the boat. The men stopped struggling.

From beneath the deck came a loud crunching. The sailors staggered as their little vessel rocked. They looked wildly around and then down at the hat. The strange turn of events must have something to do with the hat! The sailors fought to rid themselves of it.

But the fight ended quickly, as the deck splintered and the entire boat was pulled straight down. A giant geyser rose up from the sea, raining down wood and bits of canvas. And, in the blink of an eye, the water was still and the fishing boat was no more.

Not far away, in the headquarters of the East India Trading Company, Will Turner was escorted by two guards into the office of Lord Beckett. A large, unfinished map of the world took up one whole wall of the office.

"Those won't be necessary," Beckett said, pointing to the shackles on Will's wrists.

The guards released Will. "Do you intend to release Elizabeth, as well?" Will asked.

"That is entirely up to you," Beckett answered, and then quickly rephrased his response. "That is entirely *dependent* on you," he clarified. Beckett used his cane to stoke the room's fireplace. "We wish for you to act as our agent in a business transaction with our mutual friend, Captain Sparrow."

"More acquaintance than friend," Will said. "How do *you* know him?"

"We've had dealings in the past," Beckett said, displaying the letter *P* on the end of his glowing cane – the same *P* brand that was burned into Jack's arm. "We have each left our marks on the other."

"What mark did he leave on you?" Will asked, but Beckett did not respond. Instead he said, "By your efforts, Jack Sparrow was set free. I ask you to go to him and recover a certain property in his possession."

"Recover," Will said sceptically. "At the point of a sword?"

Beckett smiled. "Bargain," he suggested slyly. "To mutual benefit and for fair value."

He removed several large documents from his desk. They were signed by the King of England. "Letters of Marque," Beckett explained. "You will offer what amounts to a full pardon. Jack will be free, a privateer in the employ of England."

Will looked at the letters and shook his head. He knew that the Letters of Marque would give him the right to take Jack's possessions, but something didn't feel right. "For some reason, I doubt Jack will consider employment to be the same as freedom," Will pointed out.

"Jack Sparrow is a dying breed," Beckett snarled. He motioned to the map on the wall. "The world is shrinking, the blank edges of the map filled in. Jack will have to find a place in the New World, or perish.

"Not unlike you," Beckett continued, bringing the point home. "You and your fiancée face the hangman's noose. Certainly, that's motivation enough for you to convince Captain Sparrow to accept our offer. And for you to accept, as well, Mr Turner."

Will considered the proposal. "So you'll get both Jack and the *Black Pearl*?"

Beckett seemed surprised. "The *Black Pearl*? No, Mr Turner, the item in question is considerably smaller and far more valuable, something Sparrow keeps on his person at all times. A Compass."

Beckett noticed a look of recognition on Will's face.

"Ah, you know it," Beckett hissed. Then he added, "Bring back the Compass or there is no deal!"

Will Turner stormed out of Beckett's office and through the gates of the Port Royal prison. He

152

pushed past the red-coated guard and moved down the stone corridor to Elizabeth's cell. Governor Swann followed closely behind.

"Here, now!" the guard called out. "You can't be here, Mr Swann!"

"*Governor* Swann," he said, correcting the guard. "I'm not wearing this wig to keep my head warm, you know." Swann looked into the guard's face. "Carruthers, isn't it? Enjoy your job, Mr Carruthers?"

The guard quickly changed his tone. "Yes, sir. Particularly when the folks come up to visit the prisoners."

"Very good," Swann said. He nodded toward the door and the guard quickly exited.

As the governor approached the dank cell, he heard Elizabeth say to Will, "Jack's Compass? Why would Beckett want that?"

Elizabeth was behind bars, still in her wedding dress. "Does it matter?" Will asked. "I'm to find Jack and convince him to return to Port Royal. In exchange, the charge against us will be dropped."

Will stepped as close to Elizabeth as possible with bars between them. "If I hadn't set Jack free . . ." he began, trailing off regretfully. "I never expected you would bear the consequences."

Elizabeth smiled. "I share the consequences gladly." She reached through the bars and took his hands. "How are you going to find him?" she asked anxiously.

Her confidence touched Will's heart. He suddenly felt he could do anything. "Tortuga. I'll start there and not stop searching until I find him, and then I will come back here and marry you."

"Properly?" Elizabeth asked.

"Eagerly," Will promised.

Chapter 5

Will Turner started his search immediately. He would check every island in the Caribbean if he had to – he was going to find Jack. He made his way to Tortuga, stopping at various island ports on the way. On one, he walked up the dock and asked the first man he saw of Jack's whereabouts.

"Captain Jack Sparrow?" the weathered sailor answered. "Owes me four doubloons. Heard he was dead."

Down a cobblestone alley on another island, Will made his way into a candlelit tavern. The innkeeper, a square, thickset man, told Will, "Ran off with a Creole woman to Madagascar." Then he added with a wink, "She was half his age and twice his height!"

On a beach a half-blind fisherman told his version. "Singapore is what I heard. Sure as the tide," he nodded with a toothless grin, "Jack Sparrow will turn up in Singapore!"

Will sighed. There were a thousand tales about Jack Sparrow's whereabouts. Will had one last chance to get the truth – ironically, in a place where truth was hard to come by – Tortuga!

Tortuga was a well-known haunt of Captain Jack Sparrow's. It was the dirtiest port in all the Caribbean; a place for drunken pirates on the lookout for fresh risks and high adventure. A place, Will remembered as the stench of Tortuga filled his nostrils, Jack held dear to his heart.

As soon as Will arrived, he saw a woman he had met the last time he had been to Tortuga with Jack. The woman had red hair and wore a red dress. Her name, if he remembered correctly, was Scarlett. He asked her if she'd seen Jack recently.

"I haven't seen him in a month," Scarlett snapped. "When you find him, give him a message." She raised her hand and struck Will across the face before stalking off.

Rubbing his cheek as he walked on, Will noticed a shrimper on the deck of a small boat.

"Can't say 'bout Jack Sparrow," the shrimper told Will as he pulled in his nets. "But there's an island just south of the straits where I trade spice for delicious long pork. No, can't say for Jack, but you'll find a ship there, a ship with black sails."

For a few coins, Will convinced the shrimper to sail him out to the island. As they came around the point, Will saw it for himself; the *Black Pearl* careened onto the sand! His spirits soared.

"My brother, he will row you to shore," the shrimper told Will. He gave a taller, round-faced man a nod as Will climbed into his tiny rowing boat. But halfway to the beach, the brother told Will, "No," and began to turn the boat around.

"What's wrong?" Will asked. "The beach is right there." But the man only rowed faster back toward the shrimp boat.

Will had no choice. He shook his head, dived in and swam to the shore.

Soaking wet, Will walked over the beach towards the *Black Pearl*. The huge ship rested, wedged into the sand. No noise came from her decks.

A bit further on, Will found the remains of a campfire. He felt the ashes. They were still warm. Jack must have been here. He had to be close!

"Jack!" Will called out. "Jack Sparrow! Mister Gibbs! Anyone . . ."

Will turned towards the dense jungle and saw a flutter in the branches. It was Cotton's parrot!

"Good to see a familiar face," Will said to the old bird, now even surer Jack and the crew were on the island.

"Don't eat me!" the parrot squawked.

"I'm not even hungry," Will said as he looked for a path through the jungle.

"DON'T EAT ME!" the parrot screamed even louder.

Will turned his attention back to the bird. "Look, you're nothing but feathers and bones and you probably taste like pigeon." The parrot went silent.

"Sorry," Will said, feeling guilty. "That was uncalled for. Listen . . . if anyone should ask, tell them Will Turner went into the jungle in search of Jack Sparrow. Understand?" Will sighed. "I'm talking to a parrot," he said to himself.

"Aye, aye, sir!" the parrot answered, bobbing his head.

Will grinned, drew his sword and began hacking into the jungle. He cut through the huge leaf of a palm and noticed a small, red flask on the jungle floor. "Gibbs . . ." Will said quietly, recognizing the old pirate's flask.

He crouched down to pick it up and noticed a trip wire was attached. Will smiled, thinking the pirates had set a trap. Holding on to the wire he followed it to a tree. Suddenly, two eyes appeared in the tree trunk as a perfectly camouflaged arm reached out and yanked the trip wire hard.

In an instant, Will was pulled off his feet and dangled upside down. As he hung by his leg, he saw a group of the island's warriors. They had bite marks all over their faces and bodies, and were wearing what looked like human bones! No wonder the shrimper had been so frightened. The warriors lunged at him with their spears raised. Will kicked off the tree and knocked several of them to the ground.

"Come on!" Will said, provoking one warrior. "I'm right here!"

The warrior raised a blowgun and fired a dart into Will's neck. Will went limp and the warrior cut him down.

Chapter 6

Meanwhile, in a dank cell in Port Royal, Elizabeth could do nothing but wait. Moonlight poured through the cell's small window and cast shadows on the wall. She was exhausted and had just closed her eyes when she heard the jangle of keys.

"Come quickly!" she heard a voice that sounded like her father's call out. Governor Swann stepped out from the shadows.

"What's happening?" Elizabeth asked. The guard swung open the door and Elizabeth hurried out of her cell. Governor Swann gave the guard a nod.

"I've arranged passage for you back to England," Governor Swann said as he and his daughter ran quickly down a torchlit corridor. "The captain is an old friend."

The governor led Elizabeth to a waiting

carriage, but Elizabeth refused to get in. She was waiting for Will.

"We cannot count on Will's help," the governor said desperately, drawing a pistol. "Beckett has offered only one pardon. One. And it has been promised to Sparrow. Do not ask me to endure the sight of my daughter walking to the gallows! Do not!" He pushed her inside and pressed the pistol into her hand. Then he shut the door and hastily drove the carriage to the waiting ship.

As they neared the dock, the governor slowed his horses to a stop. Two men stood huddled in the shadows. One of them wore a captain's hat.

"Stay inside," the governor said to Elizabeth as he leapt down. He hurried over to the two men. "Captain Hawkins!" the governor said, relieved to see a friend.

But Hawkins did not answer. The other man stepped away and the captain slumped forward, his tunic covered in blood. Governor Swann suddenly realized that the other man in the shadows had been holding the captain's body upright.

"Evening, Governor," the man said, slowly wiping the blood from his knife with a handkerchief. Swann gasped. He recognized the man. It was Mercer, Beckett's clerk.

"Shame, that," Mercer said as he motioned toward the body. Governor Swann bolted toward the carriage in a panic. "Elizabeth!" he cried out. But, with a whistle, Mercer had a company of troops assembled.

Mercer smiled and yanked the carriage door open himself. It was empty.

"Where is she?" Mercer demanded angrily.

"Who?" Swann asked.

Mercer slammed the governor against the carriage and snarled, "Elizabeth!"

"She was always a wilful child," the governor offered innocently. Mercer ordered the man to be put in irons and, with a violent jerk, led him away.

Chapter 7

Lord Beckett entered his dark office inside the East India Trading Company building. He lit a lamp on his large mahogany desk and noticed that the case that held the Letters of Marque was empty. He also sensed that he was not alone.

Elizabeth stepped from the shadows and raised the pistol her father had given her. "These Letters of Marque," Elizabeth said, slapping the documents on his desk. "They are signed by the king, but blank."

Beckett smiled, unafraid. "And not valid until they bear my signature and seal."

"I have information," Elizabeth said, the gun steady in her hand. "You sent Will to get you the Compass owned by Jack Sparrow. It will do you no good. I have been to *Isla de Muerta*. I have seen the treasure myself. There is something you need to know."

Beckett smiled smugly. "Ah, I see. You think the Compass points only to *Isla de Muerta*. I am afraid you are mistaken, Miss Swann. I care not for cursed Aztec Gold." He recalled the treasure trove in the cave where Jack defeated Barbossa. "My desires are not so provincial."

Lord Beckett motioned to a huge world map. "There is more than one chest of value in these waters," he said. "So perhaps you wish to enhance your offer . . ."

Elizabeth drew the hammer back on the pistol and levelled it at Lord Beckett's head. He suddenly stopped laughing.

"Consider into your calculations that you robbed me of my wedding night," Elizabeth said sternly.

At gunpoint, Beckett signed the papers, but he did not immediately hand them over.

"You are making great effort to ensure Sparrow's freedom," Beckett said, curious.

"These are not going to Jack," Elizabeth replied.

"Then to ensure Mr Turner's freedom. And what about me? I'll still want the Compass. Consider that in your calculations."

With that, Beckett released his hold on the Letters of Marque. Elizabeth now had what she had come for. She turned and disappeared into the dark.

The following morning, a merchant vessel, the *Edinburgh Trader*, sailed from Port Royal. As the ship moved into open water, a sailor on deck came upon something strange. He picked it up; it was a wedding dress.

Captain Bellamy heard the commotion and immediately came on deck. His bursar and quartermaster were trying to pull the dress from each other's grip.

"If both of you fancy the dress," Captain Bellamy shouted, "you'll just have to share, and wear it one after the other."

"It's not like that, sir," the bursar answered swiftly. "The ship is haunted!"

Bellamy looked at the dress. "Is it, now?"

"Aye," the quartermaster agreed. "There's a female presence here with us, sir . . . everyone feels it."

The crew began to grumble. "Ghost of a lady widowed before her marriage, I figure it," a sailor said and spat neatly, "searching for her husband lost at sea."

The bursar nodded. "We need to throw it overboard and hope the spirit follows, or this ship will taste the icy waters in a fortnight, mark my words!"

A sailor painting the rail listened closely to the argument.

"Enough!" Captain Bellamy ordered. He took the dress and examined it closely. "Men, this appears to me nothing more as we have a stowaway on board. A young woman, by the looks of it. To your duties. And if there is a stowaway and 'tis a woman, I don't see she's likely to escape without notice, aye?"

The crew considered this for a moment and then scattered, all searching for the lady. The sailor who was painting the rail turned to face the rest of the crew.

But it wasn't a sailor at all. It was Elizabeth, well disguised in sailor's clothes. She put down her paintbrush and joined the search for the lady, all but unnoticed by the rowdy gang.

Chapter 8

Meanwhile, in a distant jungle, Will Turner awoke to find himself tied up and being paraded through a small village filled with huts. The island's inhabitants watched the procession with curiosity. Finally, Will was set down before a huge throne.

He looked up . . . and smiled. Sitting on the throne, dressed in ornate ceremonial garb, was none other than Captain Jack Sparrow!

"Jack Sparrow," Will said. "I can honestly say I am glad to see you."

Jack didn't respond. He just stared blankly at Will. It was as though he had never seen Will before.

The warriors pushed Will forward. "Jack? Jack, it's me, Will Turner. Tell them to let me go."

Jack stepped down from his throne and gave Will's arm a pinch. He spoke in a language Will had never heard. The warriors nodded. Will suddenly noticed that the throne was no ordinary throne – it was made of human bones.

"Jack, listen," Will said desperately. "The Compass. That's all I need. Jack, Elizabeth is in danger. We were arrested for helping *you*. She faces the gallows!"

Motioning toward Will's leg, one of the warriors hungrily rubbed his belly, suggesting that Will would make a fine meal. Jack nodded and the tribe cheered.

"No!" Will shouted as the warriors grabbed him. "Jack, what did you tell them?" But Jack didn't answer. He climbed back on his throne and stared off into the distance.

As the warriors dragged Will past Jack to prepare him for dinner, Jack's eyes rolled wildly in his head, catching Will's attention. "Save me!" Jack whispered desperately out of the corner of his mouth.

The warriors dragged Will to a chasm where two cages made from bones hung from thick rope. Will noticed that some of the crew of the *Black Pearl* were trapped in the cages. Before Will could react, he was tossed into a cage.

"Ah, Will, you shouldn't have come!" Gibbs shouted in greeting.

Will struggled to his feet, then reached into his pocket. He handed Gibbs the flask he had found on the jungle floor. Gibbs raised it as Will asked about Jack's odd behaviour and leader status over the tribe.

"Why would he do this to you?" Will asked, looking around at the caged crew. "If Jack is the chief . . ."

"Aye," Gibbs answered dismally, "the Pelegostos made Jack their chief, but he stays chief for only so long as he *acts* like a chief . . . which means he cannot do anything they think a chief ought not do."

"He's a captive, then," Will said, "as much as any of us."

Gibbs frowned. "Worse, as it turns out. The Pelegostos believe that Jack is a god, trapped in human form. They intend to do Jack the honour of releasing him from his fleshy prison."

Out of the corner of his eye, Will noticed Cotton add his two cents. He mimed something about being cut up with a knife. Will frowned.

"They'll roast and eat him. It's a deeply

held religious belief," Gibbs mused. "Or, we figure, maybe they just get awful hungry."

Will could see most of the crew between the two cages, but a good many pirates were gone. "Where's the rest of the crew?" he asked.

"These cages we're in," Gibbs sighed, "wasn't built till after we got here."

Will looked at the cages of human bone and quickly removed his hand.

"The feast starts when the sun sets," Gibbs said gravely. "Jack's life will end . . . when the drums stop."

Chapter 9

In a small boat just offshore, two pirates in worn clothing, Pintel and Ragetti, rowed with their backs to the setting sun. The bumbling duo was all that remained of Barbossa's crew. Ragetti, the tall thin one, held a book in his lap. ". . . and I say it was divine providence what escaped us from jail," he said, adjusting his wooden eye.

"And I say it was me being clever," Pintel, the shorter one, replied. A dog with a ring of keys in its mouth suddenly raised its head at the bow. Pintel patted the dog on the head. "Ain't that right, poochie?"

"How do you know it wasn't Divine Providence what inspired you to be clever?" Ragetti argued. "Anyways, I ain't stealing no ship."

"It ain't stealing," Pintel said as they neared the point of the small island. "It's salvaging, and since when did you care?"

"Now that we're not immortal no more," Ragetti said nervously, "we need to take care of our immortal souls." He looked down at the book in his lap.

"You know you can't read!" Pintel shouted at him.

"It's the Bible," the wooden-eyed pirate Ragetti said, smiling, his teeth broken and brown. "You get credit for trying."

"Pretending to read the Bible is a lie, and that's a mark against ya," Pintel yelled, when the *Black Pearl* suddenly came into view. They'd been looking for it for what seemed like forever, and now . . .

"Look! There it is!" Pintel cried.

The dog suddenly jumped into the clear blue water and swam for shore. "What's got into him?" Pintel asked.

"Must have spotted a *cat*fish," Ragetti chuckled.

As they reached the shore, Pintel looked up at the ship's black sails. "It's ours for the taking!" he said greedily, as the sound of drums began to sound through the jungle and out to the sandy beach.

Chapter 10

The beat of the drums was building as the Pelegostos prepared for their grand feast. As they gathered wood for the fire pit, their guest of honour and main course, Captain Jack Sparrow, nodded his approval and tried to force a smile. "I notice women here, but very few children – why is that? Are the little ones most tasty?" he asked.

Jack didn't get an answer. The warriors were busy placing a large spit over the fire pit. Jack gulped and took a breath. "Not big enough!" he shouted, boldly striding towards the pit, pretending to act more like a chief in order to buy himself more time.

He frowned and shook his head as the Pelegostos stared. "Not big enough!" he said, widening his arms. *"I am the chief! I need more wood! Big fire!"* he said in the language of the Pelegostos. "MORE WOOD!"

The warriors dropped their spears and hurried away to find wood enough to satisfy their chief. Jack stood tall, his arms folded over his chest, and glowered until every warrior was gone. Then he took off like a shot.

Stumbling across a bridge of twisted vines, he ran past a group of huts. Suddenly finding himself at the edge of a steep cliff and about to fall right over, Jack began waving his arms in a panic. Righting himself, he ran to the nearest hut.

"Rope, long rope," he said, rummaging frantically through the uninhabited hut.

He found a box of spices with the East India Trading Company insignia on it. Jack was about to toss it aside when a huge warrior appeared in the hut's doorway. Jack stepped back and looked into the warrior's fearsome face.

"Not running away, nooo . . ." Jack said, opening the box of spices. He took a handful and rubbed it on his body. "See?"

Jack soon found himself dusted nicely with a coating of fresh spices and tied to the enormous spit, hanging over a huge pile of kindling wood set in a large pit. He sighed and looked down at the fire pit, which now, thanks to his own efforts, was huge. "Nice job," he said, nodding to the proud warriors. Too nice, he added silently to himself.

Meanwhile, inside their cages, the pirates waited helplessly. But Will Turner wasn't about to give up. Elizabeth's life was at stake – he had to get to Jack. "Swing your cage," he yelled to the men as he shifted his weight from side to side, causing the cage to rock. "Get to the wall!"

Leech and the pirates in the other cage got the idea. They rocked their cage to the side of the steep chasm wall and grabbed a vine. "Put your feet through," Will shouted. "Start to climb!"

Pulling with all their might and grabbing for footholds, the crew members slowly moved the two cages up the wall.

A guard passed and stared at the tilted cages. Every man instantly froze. But, after a moment, Leech's men tried to move up an inch. The guard noticed. With a loud scream he sent out the alarm. The drums stopped.

Inside the village, Jack, tied up like a turkey, heard the alarm just as a torch was about to light the pit. The guard suddenly burst into the village, screaming and pointing to the jungle. His meaning was clear – the prisoners were escaping!

"*After them!*" Jack ordered, still trying to appear in charge. He jerked his head toward the jungle. "*Don't let them get away!*"

The warriors hesitated, not knowing whether to light the fire or run. After all, it was their duty to release their god from his fleshy prison. But it was also their god who was commanding them to leave. They finally ran off, tossing the torch to the ground as they left.

Jack's eyes grew wide as the torch slowly rolled toward the pit beneath him. Suddenly, a twig at the edge of the pit caught fire. As the entire pit went up in flames with a giant *whoosh*, Jack tried to blow out the fire. But it was no use. Captain Jack Sparrow was as good as cooked!

Captain Jack is back for another adventure on
the high seas.

Elizabeth Swann's wedding day is ruined.

Lord Beckett has put Elizabeth in jail, and Will
promises he will rescue her.

Will Turner sails off to find Captain Jack Sparrow.

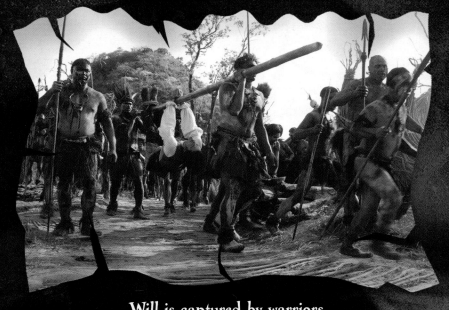

Will is captured by warriors.

The warriors have a new leader – Captain Jack!

Elizabeth Swann disguises herself as a sailor.

Will listens while Tia Dalma tells them the story of Davy Jones.

Jack sneaks away. He needs to leave Tortuga and find Jones's chest.

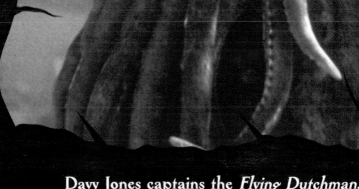

Davy Jones captains the *Flying Dutchman*

Will shows his father, Bootstrap Bill,
a picture of Davy Jones's key.

Pirates Pintel and Ragetti have stolen
Davy Jones's chest!

Chapter 11

Meanwhile, back in the chasm, Will's cage reached the top first. In the other cage, Leech reached for a thick vine, but screamed as the vine came twisting *into* the cage. Leech had pulled on a giant snake, not a vine! The pirates quickly let go and the vine that had been holding them snapped from the weight of the jerking motion. The cage plummeted to the floor of the deep chasm with a crash!

Will heard the men's screams just as he rolled his cage up and out of the chasm. But he didn't have time to worry about Leech and the others. The warriors were racing straight toward his own cage.

With no way to escape, Will and the others pulled the cage up around their legs and began to run through the jungle with their feet sticking out of the bottom of the cage. They had to get to the *Pearl* – fast!

*   *   *

Back in the village, Jack was trying to move fast, too. He was desperately trying to bounce the spit up and down and completely away from the fire. A boy from the village watched as the bouncing pirate choked and sputtered over the flames.

Jack finally bounced high enough and fell away from the pit, gasping for air. He managed to stand upright and ran with the spit on his back as fast as his scorched feet would allow.

The boy who had witnessed Jack's escape ran into the jungle. He caught up with the warriors and told them that Jack had hopped away. The raging warriors howled and took off again. But now they weren't after Jack's crew – they were after Jack himself!

Not far away, Will and his portion of the crew had broken free from their cage and had arrived on the beach to find the *Pearl* already prepared. While the warriors had been busy chasing everyone around the island, Pintel and Ragetti had been getting ready to steal the ship. Luckily for Jack's crew, that made for a fast getaway!

Gibbs was the first aboard. "Excellent!" he called out, seeing the *Black Pearl* ready to make sail. "Our work's half done."

The crew barged past Pintel and Ragetti without a second look and took their positions on deck. "Boys, make ready to sail!" Gibbs shouted.

Will worked alongside Gibbs. "What about Jack? I won't leave without him."

Gibbs suddenly pointed to the beach in horror. Will looked up and saw Jack racing down the beach with a hoard of warriors at his heels.

"Jack! Hurry!" Gibbs shouted. Jack *was* hurrying. The wily captain had managed to get free of the spit. With his arms flailing about, he was trying to stay ahead of the warriors.

Gibbs turned to the crew. "Cast off! Cast off!"

On the beach, the Prison Dog, which had made it to dry land after abandoning Pintel and Ragetti, appeared and began growling at the warriors.

"Good doggy!" Jack shouted. He sloshed through the surf to the side of the *Pearl* and Gibbs quickly hauled him aboard.

The dog barked, holding the warriors at bay until the *Black Pearl* disappeared into the horizon. Suddenly, the dog seemed to sense it was in trouble. It stopped barking, wagged its tail a few times, looked at the warriors – the very hungry warriors – then turned and made a run for it.

Chapter 12

Jack Sparrow sat on the deck of the *Black Pearl*, catching his breath.

"Put as much distance between us and this island and make for open sea?" Gibbs asked him.

"Yes to the first and yes to the second, but only insofar as we keep to the shallows . . ." Jack replied, still panting.

Gibbs frowned. "That seems a bit contradictory, sir."

Jack nodded. "I have every faith in your reconciliatory navigational skills, Mr Gibbs," Jack said, matter of factly.

Then he moved to the rail, opened his Compass and stared at its face. He was so focused that he didn't notice he had company. Will Turner stood right beside him.

"Jack," Will said quietly.

"Not now," Jack answered, without looking up.

"Jack, I need . . ."

"Not *now*," Jack snapped, reaching for his pistol. Finally he looked up at Will. "Oh. You. Where's that monkey?" Jack asked, thinking that as long as he had his pistol handy, he might as well practise. High in the rigging, the monkey let out a teasing screech.

"Jack," Will said once again, trying to get the captain's attention. "I need that Compass."

"Why?" Jack asked, taking another look before snapping it shut.

"To rescue Elizabeth," Will said.

Jack shook his head and began to climb the rigging. "That has a familiar ring to it," he said. He was right. The last time Will had found himself in the company of Jack, it had been when he was trying to rescue Elizabeth. To drive the point home, Jack added, "Have you considered keeping a more watchful eye on her? Maybe just lock her up somewhere?"

"She *is* locked up. In prison. Bound to hang for helping you," Will snapped.

Jack paused for a moment as Will's words sunk in. Then he shrugged and continued to climb. "There comes a time when one must take responsibility for one's mistakes," Jack said as he settled into the ship's crow's nest.

Suddenly, Jack felt the cold touch of steel at his throat. It was Will's sword.

"You will hand it over. Now!" he said, leaning into the crow's nest. "In exchange, you will be granted full pardon and commissioned as a privateer in service to England."

Jack sighed. "I wonder, what will my crew think when they see you've skewered their beloved and duly chosen captain?"

"I think they will see it as an example," Will told him sternly.

"All right," Jack nodded. "You get the Compass, you rescue your bonnie lass. Where's my profit?"

"You get full pardon," Will explained. "Freedom. A commission."

Jack shook his head. "No, accepting those things is what *you* want from *me*. Don't you want to know what *I* want from *you*?"

Will lowered his sword and turned his head away. Nothing was stickier than negotiating with a blasted pirate. "What do you want from me, Jack?" Will said finally, giving in.

"It's quite dangerous . . ." Jack said, cautioning Will. "I will trade you the Compass, if you will recover for me . . ." he fumbled for the small piece of cloth in his pocket, ". . . this."

Will eyed the imprint of the key on the cloth. "So you get my favour *and* the Letters of Marque as well?" Leave it to Jack Sparrow to come away on the upside of a tricky bargain, Will thought.

Jack nodded. "And you save fair damsel."

"*This* is going to save Elizabeth?" Will said, looking at the cloth.

Jack leaned in towards Will as if the very air were listening. "How much do you know about Davy Jones?" he asked in a whisper.

"Nothing," Will said.

"Yep," Jack said, nodding firmly, "it's going to save Elizabeth."

Chapter 13

Elsewhere on the ocean, a figure slipped silently across the ratline of the *Edinburgh Trader*. It was Elizabeth Swann, still dressed in the clothes of a sailor. She moved towards the light of the captain's cabin, where she could hear voices raised in an argument.

"It's an outrage!" Captain Bellamy complained, looking at the ship's accounts. "Port tariffs, berthing fees and, heaven help me, *pilotage*!"

"I'm afraid, sir, Tortuga is the only free port left in these waters," the ship's quartermaster said, knowing the captain was bound to respond.

And respond he did. Bellamy was furious. "A *pirate* port is what you mean! Well, I'm sorry, but an honest sailor I am. I make my living square, and sleep well each night, thank you."

He didn't get to continue. "Sir!" the bursar interrupted, pointing to the cabin window.

"What?" Bellamy demanded angrily. But the bursar was shaking so hard he could only point. The captain turned to see a shadowy white dress float by the cabin window. He ran out onto the dimly lit deck.

"Tell me you do see that," the ship's cook asked, terrified.

"Aye, I do see that," Bellamy answered as he watched the white gown float to the bowsprit. High up in the rigging, Elizabeth secretly pulled the dress along by a fishing line. With a whisk of her arm, she pulled a line that raised the arm of the dress. It pointed to Captain Bellamy, then out to sea. His crew immediately shuffled away from him.

"She wants you to do something," the bursar said.

"Jump overboard?" the quartermaster asked quickly.

Bellamy tossed him a scowl. "She's trying to give a sign!"

Then, on the sea winds, a soft voice whispered, "Tor . . . tu . . . ga."

"Did you hear that?" the cook exclaimed.

"Ber-mu-da?" the bursar said.

"Tobago?" the quartermaster suggested.

Suddenly, the ghostly bride raced toward the rail and dropped over the side. As the crew was busy looking overboard, Elizabeth dropped down behind them.

"Look for a sign!" Bellamy shouted to his men.

"There!" the quartermaster said, pointing out to sea. "There it is! There's the sign!"

"That's seaweed," a sailor pointed out.

"Seaweed can be a sign," the quartermaster argued.

Elizabeth lost all patience. She grabbed the shoulder of the bursar and turned him around. "What's that over there?" she said in a low, deep voice.

On the deck, the word 'Tortuga' was burning in lamp oil.

"Is it telling us to go there?" the terrified quartermaster asked.

Elizabeth was about to burst with frustration, when Captain Bellamy spoke up. "Men," he said. "What say ye to a course change? Prudence suggests we make way for the island of Tortuga!"

As the crew shouted their approval, Elizabeth pulled her sailor's cap down lower over her face and smiled. Her plan had worked. Now, all she could do was wait.

Chapter 14

Elizabeth was heading to Tortuga to find Will, but Will was nowhere near Tortuga. He was with Jack Sparrow, heading inland.

Through a heavy mist, two longboats from the *Black Pearl* rowed to the mouth of the Pantano River. Will, Ragetti and Gibbs rode in the lead, followed by Jack, Pintel and Cotton. Next to Cotton was a cage covered with a length of canvas.

As they rowed past thick tangles of twisted roots and bark, Will quietly asked Gibbs the question the whole crew wanted to know. "What is it that has Jack so spooked?"

Gibbs heaved a sigh. "Jack has run afoul of none other than Davy Jones himself," he said gravely. "Thinks he is only safe on land. If he goes out to open water, he'll be taken."

"By Davy Jones?" Will asked in disbelief. Jack never seemed scared of anyone.

"Well, I'll tell ye. If you believe such things, there's a beast does the bidding of Davy Jones. A fearsome creature from the depths, with giant tentacles that'll suction your face clean off, and drag an entire ship down to the crushing darkness. The Kraken," Gibbs said, shuddering at the very name of the evil thing. "They say the stench of its breath . . ." Gibbs stopped, not wanting to go on, and Will could see real fear in the old pirate's eyes. "If you believe such things," he repeated with a tilt of his head, and kept rowing.

Will glanced back at Jack, who was nervously picking at a hangnail. "Never thought Jack the type to be afraid of dying."

"Aye, but with Jones, it ain't about the dying – it's about the punishment," Gibbs answered. "Think of the worst fate you can conjure for yourself, stretching on forever . . . and that's what awaits you in Davy Jones's locker."

For a moment, everyone on the longboat was silent as they pondered Gibbs's words.

"And the key will spare him that?" Will finally asked.

"Now, that's the very question Jack wants

answered," Gibbs whispered, looking over at the captain. "Bad enough, even, to go visit . . . *her*."

"Her?" Will said nervously.

"Aye," Gibbs nodded.

As the boats rowed into the still water of a steamy bayou, fireflies flickered in the heavy air. The longboats pulled up to a rope ladder that hung down from a sprawling wooden shack high up in a tree. A lantern hung at the door, casting a dim glow on the cautious pirate crew. They had arrived. Now the question was, where?

"No worries, mates," Jack said, trying to sound lighthearted. He grabbed the ladder. "I'll handle this. Tia Dalma and I go way back. Thick as thieves. Nigh inseparable, we were, er, have been . . . before."

"I'll watch your back," Gibbs volunteered.

"It's me front I'm worried about," Jack muttered.

With one last nervous glance around, Jack pushed his way into the shack, the rest of his crew sticking close behind. As their eyes adjusted to the low light, they saw all manner of strange creatures in jars and bottles. Some were stuffed and hanging from the rafters. Others moved around in jars of murky water. Overhead dangled an old, dusty crocodile. Ragetti noticed a jar of eyeballs in a corner and put a hand over his eye socket that was plugged with a wooden eyeball.

At a table, in the shadows, sat Tia Dalma, a mystic with an eye keener than any pirate's. She'd been hovering over crab claws when her head suddenly snapped up. She stood. "Jack Sparrow," she said. "I always knew the wind was going to blow you back to me one day."

Her eyes moved past Jack and landed on Will. She smiled as she looked at him. "You have a touch of destiny in you, William Turner," she said, moving closer.

"You know me?" Will asked, confused.

"You want to know me," she replied in riddle, staring into Will's eyes.

"There will be no knowing here," Jack announced, walking over to Tia Dalma and ushering her back towards the table. "We came here for help."

As the pirates gathered around the table, Tia Dalma pulled Will in close. "Asking for help does not sound like Jack Sparrow."

"It's not so much for me," Jack answered

coolly, "as for William, so he can earn a favour from me."

Tia Dalma nodded. "Now *that* sounds like Jack Sparrow. What service may I do you? You know I demand payment."

"I brought payment!" Jack said brightly, taking the cage from Pintel's hand. He raised the canvas, revealing Jack the monkey trapped inside. Jack raised his pistol and shot it. The angry little monkey barely blinked. He just glared back.

"See?" Jack exclaimed. He glanced up at the ceiling. "Perhaps you can give it the crocodile treatment?"

Tia Dalma stood and opened the cage.

Gibbs moaned as the monkey raced through the shack. "You don't know how long it took us to catch that," he said sadly.

"The payment is fair," she said, ignoring Gibbs. Her eyes wandered again to Will.

Jack produced the drawing of the key from his pocket and passed it to Will, who quickly showed it to Tia Dalma. "We're looking for this . . . and what it goes to," Will said.

"That Compass you bartered from me can't lead you to this?" Tia Dalma asked.

"No," Jack answered flatly.

Tia Dalma laughed and turned her attention back to Will as she spoke to Jack. "Your key goes to a chest . . . and it is what lies inside the chest you seek, isn't it?"

"What is inside?" Gibbs asked.

"Gold? Jewels? Unclaimed properties of a valuable nature?" Pintel said hopefully.

"Nothing bad, I hope," Ragetti said, still unnerved by it all.

Chapter 15

Tia Dalma smiled at the pirates that surrounded her, as if they were small children. Then she began to tell her tale. "You know of Davy Jones, yes? A man of the sea, a great sailor until he ran afoul of that which vexes all men."

"What vexes all men?" Will asked her.

She smiled. "What, indeed?"

"The sea," Gibbs said solemnly.

Tia Dalma shook her head.

"Sums," Pintel said.

The gypsy shook her head again.

"The dichotomy of good and evil," Ragetti suggested. Everyone in the room looked at the one-eyed pirate and shook their heads.

"A woman," Jack said, ending the game.

Tia Dalma smiled at the rough pirate. "A woman. He fell in love. It was a woman, as changing and harsh and untameable as the sea. He never stopped loving her, but the pain it caused him was too much to live with . . . but not enough to cause him to die."

They each nodded sadly, understanding the story all too well.

"Exactly *what* did he put into the chest?" Will asked.

Tia Dalma sighed. "It was not worth feeling what small, fleeting joy life brings, he decided, and so he carved out his heart, locked it away in a chest and hid the chest from the world. The key . . . he keeps with him at all times."

Will nodded, understanding. The key would open the chest that held Jones's heart.

"That was a roundabout way to get to the answer," Jack observed.

"Sauce for the gander, Jack," Tia Dalma replied with a wink.

"You knew this," Will said realizing that Jack had made a deal based on more information than he'd been willing to reveal.

"No, I didn't. I didn't know where the key was . . ." Jack stuttered, interrupting Will's thoughts.

Will rolled his eyes.

"But now we do," Jack said smoothly, "so all that is left is to slip aboard Jones's ship, the *Flying Dutchman*, take the key and then you can go back to Port Royal and save your bonnie lass."

Jack headed for the door but, before he could open it, Tia Dalma said, "Let me see your hand."

Jack hesitated. Slowly, he unwrapped his palm. Tia Dalma nodded respectfully at the sight of the Black Spot that made Jack a marked man.

Gibbs leaned in and saw the mark, too. Pintel and Ragetti watched the old pirate turn three times and spit for luck. Not knowing why, they did the same, just in case.

They watched Tia Dalma move across the room in her long, ragged dress and climb the stairs. At the top, she opened a great carved door. The sound of the ocean whispered from it. Tia Dalma slowly closed the door and descended the stairs. In her hands she carried a jar, which she handed to Jack. "Davy Jones cannot make port, cannot step on land, but once every ten years," she said to him. Leaning down, she scooped dirt into the jar. "Land is where you are safe, Jack Sparrow, and so you will carry land with you."

Jack looked into the jar. "This is a jar of dirt," Jack said, unimpressed.

"Yes."

"Is the jar of dirt going to help?" he asked sceptically.

Tia Dalma reached for the jar. "If you don't want it, give it back."

"No!" Jack cried, clutching it to his chest.

"Then it helps," she said, nodding.

Will faced Tia Dalma. "It seems we have a need to find the *Flying Dutchman*," he said. Tia Dalma smiled into his young face, then sat again at her table. Scooping up the crab claws, she tossed them down, casting a spell to reveal the direction. The claws did their job well. The crew was on its way to find Davy Jones.

Chapter 16

The *Black Pearl* sailed to an archipelago in the Caribbean that matched the outline of the claws on Tia Dalma's table. And there, on the shoals, lay a ship, the main deck slanted into the sea.

Under the glow of an old oil lantern, Jack and Gibbs silently stared at the broken vessel.

"That's the *Flying Dutchman*?" Will asked them. "She doesn't look like much."

"Neither do you," Jack snapped. "Don't underestimate her." He turned to Will. "What's your plan?" he asked.

"I row over and search the ship until I find your bloody key," Will retorted.

"If there are crewmen?" Jack asked, testing him.

"I cut down anyone in my path."

Jack smiled. "I like it. Simple and easy to remember."

Will nodded. His eyes travelled to the cloth Jack held tightly in his hand. "I bring you the key, you give me the Compass."

"Yes, and if you do get captured, just say, 'Jack Sparrow sent me to settle his debt,'" Jack ordered. Then he added, "It might save your life."

Will nodded his farewells and climbed over the rail to a waiting longboat.

As Will rowed with his back to the scuttled ship, Jack watched silently. Then he ordered Gibbs to lower the lights.

One by one, the lanterns of the *Black Pearl* went as dark as her black sails. She was all but invisible, except for the smile of one gold-toothed Captain Jack Sparrow.

Will reached the main deck of the broken ship and lit a lantern of his own. The ship seemed deserted. Bodies of seamen, all dead, were strewn haphazardly across the deck. Will felt his legs go weak as he took in the chaos around him. What had he got himself into?

Suddenly, a pulley creaked. Will turned to see a wounded sailor weakly trying to raise a sail.

"Hoist the inner jib. Bring up with a round turn. Captain's orders," the man muttered.

"Sailor, there's no use," Will said. "You've run aground."

But the beaten man kept trying. "No . . . beneath us . . . foul breath . . . waves took Billy and Quentin . . . captain's orders!"

A wave suddenly shook the ship and out of the rigging dropped a dead sailor. Will jumped back as the body hit the deck. On the sailor's back, Will could see round suction marks. He turned the body over. The man's face was gone, completely suctioned off.

The Kraken! Gibbs's description of the sea monster came rushing back to Will.

Will quickly backed away from the body. He looked over the rail in a panic and saw nothing but the rolling blackness of the sea. An eerie calm suddenly settled on the waters. Then, almost as quickly, the wind picked up to a gale. The sea churned white and, rising from the foam like a great whale breaking the surface, came an awesome ship of great power. The *Flying Dutchman*.

Will had been tricked. In order to bait the real *Flying Dutchman*, Jack had sent Will aboard a wrecked vessel. But now the ship – and its captain, Davy Jones – had arrived.

It was unlike any ship Will had ever seen. It was made of pallid wood and bones, and completely covered in items from the sea – coral, shells and seaweed. With a splash, it slammed down into the ocean, the skeleton of a winged female attached to the bow. Will hid himself behind one of the wrecked ship's cannons, but it did him no good.

From the shadows, the *Dutchman's* crew boarded the ship. They were a hideous-looking bunch. Some had scales, while others were covered in barnacles. Will pulled his sword and broke cover. He ran for the longboat, but the *Dutchman's* first mate, a man with a coral-encrusted face, named Maccus, stopped him. The rest of the crew soon joined Maccus, surrounding Will.

"Down on your marrowbones and pray!" Greenbeard, the Bo'sun, snarled through the seaweed that covered his face.

For a moment, Will stood frozen by the sight of Jones's crew. But as soon as he regained his wits, he ran his sword through a vat of whale oil and thrust it into his lantern. His sword flamed wildly as he slashed away, searing the crewmen's watery flesh. Will spun around to attack the crew at his back when a pulley hit him squarely in the face and knocked him out cold. He was suddenly defenceless and at the mercy of the crew of the *Flying Dutchman*.

Chapter 17

When he came to, Will was still on the scuttled ship. He was part of a line of sailors, all of them on their knees. Will was the final sailor in this line. He looked off to the side and watched as someone strode on to the deck. It was Davy Jones himself – and he was as terrible as he'd been described.

The captain's dark eyes stared out from behind a long beard of octopus tentacles that moved and curled with a life of their own. He had a claw for a left hand and the fingers on his right extended out in rough tentacles, wrapping around an ivory cane. On his head he wore a black hat that resembled devil horns, and one of his legs was nothing but whalebone. With a dark glare, he looked down the line of sailors before him.

"Six men still alive," Maccus stated. "The rest have moved on."

Jones nodded and made his way down the line. "Do you fear death?" Jones asked the ship's helmsman, who appeared to be the most frightened. "I can offer you an escape," he taunted in a voice that echoed of waves crashing on a distant shore.

"Don't listen to him!" said the chaplain, who was also in the line, clutching his cross.

Jones turned and roared, "Do you not fear death?"

"I'll take my chances, sir."

"Good luck, mate," Jones said with a smirk. He nodded to Greenbeard, who tossed the man overboard.

Jones leaned close to the helmsman. His tentacled beard bristled and twisted. "You cling to the pain of life and fear death. I offer you the choice. Join my crew . . . and postpone judgment. One hundred years before the mast. Will you serve?"

The helmsman nodded quickly. "I will serve."

Jones smiled and moved down the line. At Will, he stopped and frowned. "You are neither dead nor dying. What is your purpose here?"

"Jack Sparrow sent me," Will replied, "to settle his debt."

Anger rose in Jones's face, the tentacles of his beard turning from pale pink to purple. "Did he, now?" He looked at Will for a long moment. "I am sorely tempted to accept that offer."

Jones turned his head and looked out into the darkness. It was time to take care of a little payment.

Chapter 18

ℏidden in darkness on the deck of the *Black Pearl*, Jack Sparrow looked through his spyglass and gasped. Jones was staring straight at him.

As Jack slowly lowered his telescope, Davy Jones suddenly and jarringly appeared right in front of him. The crewmen of the *Flying Dutchman* were also transported to the *Pearl*'s deck and they quickly surrounded Jack and his crew.

"You have a debt to pay," Jones said to Jack with a nasty growl. "You've been captain of the *Black Pearl* for 13 years. That was our agreement."

Jack nodded. "Technically, I was only captain for two years – then I was viciously mutinied upon."

"But a captain nonetheless," Jones replied. "Have you not introduced yourself all this time as Captain Jack Sparrow?"

"Not that I recall. Why do you ask? You have my payment. One soul, to serve on your ship. He's already over there," Jack said, referring to Will.

"You can't trade," Jones roared. "You can't substitute."

Jack raised a finger. "There is precedent regarding servitude, according to The Code of the Brethren . . ."

The tentacles on Jones's face twisted and curled. "One soul is not the same as another!"

"Ah, so we've established the proposal is sound in principle. Now we're just haggling over the price," Jack replied.

"As has been the case before, I am oddly compelled to listen to you," Jones confessed.

Jack saw his chance to bargain and pounced on it. "Just how many souls do you think my soul is worth?" he asked slyly.

Jones pondered. "One hundred souls. Three days," was the reply.

Jack flashed a sparkling grin. "You're a diamond, mate. Send me back the boy, I'll get started, right off."

"I keep the boy. A good-faith payment. That leaves you only 99 more to go."

"What?" Jack asked, astounded. "Have you

met Will Turner? He's noble and heroic, a terrific soprano – he's worth at least four. And did I mention he is in love? Due to be married. To a lovely young lady. You hate that malarkey."

Jones was not to be swayed by Jack's fancy words. "I keep the boy," he snapped. "You owe 99 souls. In three days. But I wonder, Sparrow . . . can you live with this?"

Jack considered the question briefly.

"Yep," he answered.

"You can condemn an innocent man – a friend – to a lifetime of servitude, in your name, while you roam free?" Jones asked.

"I'm good with it," Jack answered. "Shall we seal it in blood? I mean, ink?"

"Let's not, and say we did. Agreed?"

"Agreed," Jack said, still grinning. Jack looked down at his palm. The Black Spot was gone. When he looked back up, Davy Jones and his crew were gone, too.

Moments later, the *Flying Dutchman* sailed off into a distant storm with Will aboard. Jack watched silently as the ship faded from sight. He had three days to find 99 souls. There was only one place to go – Tortuga.

Chapter 19

In a corner of a crowded cantina in Tortuga, Jack sat, his feet up, Compass in hand. As Gibbs went about the business of recruiting Jack's much-needed 99 souls, Jack drank from a large mug and listened in. An unforgettable journey aboard the *Black Pearl* is what Gibbs promised a line of hopeful sailors. Of course, as it was Tortuga, every one of them was beaten and broken down.

"I've one arm and a bum leg," an old sailor told Gibbs.

"Crow's nest for you," Gibbs replied. After a few more interviews, Gibbs walked over to Jack.

"How are we doing?" Jack asked, looking up.

"Counting those four?" Gibbs sighed. "That gives us four." Gibbs worried over the number. "Nothing better happen to *me*," he added hastily.

"I make no promises," Jack said, raising an eyebrow. He was not fond of promises.

"You'd best be coming up with a new plan, Jack, and it better not be relying on that Compass. The whole crew knows it ain't worked since you was saved from the gallows."

Jack scowled as Gibbs moved back to the meagre line of recruits.

"What's your story?" Gibbs asked the next sailor. The man was drunk and unshaven, but his eyes were clear.

"My story," the man replied. "Same as your story, just one chapter behind. I became obsessed with capturing a notorious pirate . . . chased him across the seven seas. I lost all perspective, I was consumed. The pursuit cost me my crew, my commission, my life."

Gibbs took a closer look at the man. "Commodore?" he asked, suddenly recognizing him. It was Commodore Norrington – the very man who had chased Jack and the *Pearl* all the way to *Isla de Muerta*.

"Not any more," the former commodore answered. He slammed his bottle down. "So what is it? Do I make your crew or not?"

Gibbs didn't answer. He was stunned to see the fine commodore turned into a rough gentleman of fortune like himself.

The silence seemed to anger Norrington. "So, am I worthy to serve under Captain Jack Sparrow?" he roared. Then he turned and pulled his pistol. "Or should I just kill you now?" he said, aiming it across the room at Jack, who was trying to sneak away.

Jack froze and quickly forced a smile. "You're hired, mate!"

Norrington pulled the hammer back. "Sorry," he said, about to shoot anyway. "Old habits die and all that."

"Easy, soldier," a man said, grabbing Norrington's arm. "That's our captain you be threatening."

A wild shot went off and the man ducked, knocking over a table. Jack's new crew suddenly jumped up and began swinging. Pirates, out for a night of sport, joined in the brawl and swung back, tossing chairs and smashing bottles.

"Time to go," Jack said, nodding to Gibbs.

"Aye."

Jack danced through the brawl without even

a scratch. On his way out he stooped over a man who had been knocked out and tried on his hat. Too small, Jack decided, as he and Gibbs made their way to the cantina's back stairs. It was so hard to find a good hat these days, he thought to himself as the fight waged on.

As Jack and Gibbs slipped quietly away, Norrington was left with his back to a beam, slashing at the drunken hoard. "Come on, then. Do you want some British steel? You? You? You?" He was still shouting when a bottle was smashed over his head, taking him down.

Standing over him, dressed in her sailor's clothing, was Elizabeth. "I just wanted the pleasure of doing that myself," she shouted to the pirates. "Now, let's toss this mess out of here and have a drink!"

The pirates roared and tossed Norrington out to the pigs wallowing behind the cantina. Elizabeth suddenly recognized the man. And she couldn't believe her eyes.

Chapter 20

Moments later, Elizabeth rushed to the former commodore's side and knelt down. "James Norrington," she said, pitying the poor man. "What has the world done to you?"

"Nothing I didn't deserve," Norrington answered, as Elizabeth helped him to his feet.

Slowly, they made their way to the docks and stepped directly into Jack's path. "Captain Sparrow," Elizabeth said to him.

Jack looked at her. He didn't recognize her in her sailor disguise. "Come to join my crew, lad? Well enough, welcome aboard."

"I've come to find the man I love," Elizabeth declared.

Jack nodded, still not aware he was speaking to Elizabeth.

"I'm deeply flattered, son, but my first and only love is the sea," Jack replied.

"Meaning William Turner, Captain Sparrow," Elizabeth added stiffly.

"Elizabeth?" Jack said, eyeing her warily. "You know, those clothes do *not* flatter you at all."

"Jack," Elizabeth said, staying focused, "I know Will set out to find you. Where is he?"

"Darling, I am truly unhappy to have to tell you this but, through an unfortunate and entirely unforeseeable series of circumstances that have nothing whatsoever to do with me, poor Will was press-ganged into Davy Jones's crew."

"Davy Jones," Elizabeth repeated, not sure if she should believe the pirate.

"Oh, please," Norrington scoffed. "The captain of the *Flying Dutchman*? A ship that ferries those who died at sea from this world to the next . . ."

"Bang on!" Jack exclaimed. Then, recognizing Norrington, he added, "You look bloody awful, mate. What are you doing here?"

"You hired me," was his reply. "I can't help that your standards are lax."

"Jack," Elizabeth said, "all I want is to find Will."

Jack tugged at his beaded black beard for a moment before carefully replying, "Are you certain? Is that what you really want . . . most?"

"Of course," Elizabeth answered. She suddenly saw a gleam in Jack's eyes.

"I'd think you'd want to find a way to save Will . . . *most*," Jack replied.

"And you have a way to do that?"

"Well," Jack began, "there is a chest. A chest of unknown size and origin."

"What contains the still-beating heart of Davy Jones!" Pintel interjected as he passed, carrying a barrel onto the *Black Pearl*.

"Thump, THUMP!" Ragetti added, patting his hand against his chest with a grin.

Ignoring the scurvy pair, Jack quickly said, "And whoever possesses that chest possesses the leverage to command Jones to do whatever it is he – or she – wants. Including saving our brave William from his grim fate."

"How can we find it?" Elizabeth asked flatly. She didn't trust Jack, but she wanted to get to Will – soon.

Jack placed the Compass in her hand. "With this. This Compass is unique."

"Unique here having the meaning of 'broken'?" Norrington asked.

Jack tilted his head. "True enough, this Compass does not point north," he said. "It points to the thing you want most in this world."

Still sceptical, Elizabeth asked, "Jack, are you telling the truth?"

"Every word, love. What you want most in the world is to find the chest of Davy Jones, is it not?"

Elizabeth nodded. "To save Will."

Jack opened the Compass in her hand. "By finding the chest of Davy Jones," he said for emphasis. Looking at the Compass heading, he turned to Gibbs. "We have our heading!" he shouted. The *Pearl*'s crew was on its way . . . finally.

Chapter 21

Meanwhile, on the deck of the *Flying Dutchman*, Davy Jones sat playing an organ of coral that seemed to have grown from the organic moulding of the deck itself. The tune was sad and haunting and, as the notes drifted over the boat, Jones's eyes misted. His gaze was drawn to the image of a woman with flowing hair that was etched into the coral above the huge keyboard.

Elsewhere on the deck, the crew members were hard at work – including one of the newest additions, Will Turner. He was hauling a line when it suddenly slipped through his hands and a boom fell, crashing to the deck.

"Haul the weevil to his feet!" the Bo'sun shouted. In his hands he held a cat-o'-nine-tails. He slapped it against his palm. "Five from the lash'll remind you to stay on 'em!" he said, walking over to Will. But before he could take a swing,

Bootstrap Bill reached out and grabbed the crewman's wrist.

"Impeding me in my duties!" the Bo'sun snarled. "You'll share the punishment!"

"I'll take it all," Bootstrap told him.

"Will you, now?" Davy Jones asked. He had stopped playing the organ and was observing the situation carefully. "And what would prompt such an act of charity?"

Bootstrap lifted a barnacled hand, motioning toward Will. "My son. That's my son."

Jones smiled as he watched Will's eyes widen at the sight of his father. "What fortuitous circumstance be this!" Jones roared, slapping his knee. "You wish to spare your son the Bo'sun's discipline?"

"Aye," Bootstrap answered.

"Give your lash to Mr Turner. The elder," Jones ordered the Bo'sun.

Bootstrap Bill protested as the lash was placed in his hand. Being forced to lash his own son was the worst possible punishment.

"The cat's out of the bag, Mr Turner!" Jones roared. The crew cowered. "Your issue will taste its sting, be it by the Bo'sun's hand – or your own!"

The Bo'sun went to take back the lash, but Bootstrap pushed him away. He raised the lash to Will, his barnacled arm snapping forward.

Will half staggered to the hold later that night, Bootstrap following behind him. "The Bo'sun prides himself on cleaving flesh from bone with every swing," Bootstrap explained as he helped Will to a bench.

Will stared. He couldn't believe that after all these years, he was finally talking to his father.

"So I'm to understand what you did was an act of compassion?" Will asked his father.

Bootstrap nodded.

"Then I guess I am my father's son. For nearly a year, I've been telling myself that I killed you to save you," Will admitted.

"You killed me?" Bootstrap replied.

"I lifted the curse you were under, knowing it would mean your death. But at least you would no longer suffer the fate handed to you by Barbossa."

"Who is Barbossa?" Bootstrap asked blankly.

"Captain Barbossa," Will said, wondering how his father's mind could have dulled so as not to remember. "The man who led the mutiny aboard the *Black Pearl*? Who left you to live forever at the bottom of the ocean."

"Oh. Of course," Bootstrap said, nodding. His eyes misted. "It's the gift and the lie given by Jones," he told young Will. "You join the crew and think you've cheated the powers, but it's not reprieval you've found. It's oblivion. Losing what you were, bit by bit, till you end up like poor Wyvern here."

Will followed his father's eyes and noticed what looked like a carved image of an old sailor, his body part of the ship's hull.

Bootstrap sighed. "Once you've sworn an oath to the *Dutchman*, there's no leaving it. Not till your debt is paid. By then, you're not just on the ship, but of it. Why did you do it, Will?"

"I've sworn no oath," Will said truthfully.

Bootstrap's face brightened at the news. "Then you must get away."

"Not until I find this," Will said, showing his father the image of the key. "It's supposed to be on the ship. Jack wanted it; maybe it is a way out?"

Suddenly, old Wyvern moved, pulling himself free from the hold of the hull's wood. "The

Dead Man's Chest!" he moaned, his arms reaching for the cloth.

Will jumped back as the wooden creature, who had torn himself away from the body of the ship, opened his mouth and wailed. Will blanched. He knew that this was the fate for all who served Davy Jones. Old Bootstrap would soon fade into the hull, too. One more tormented soul to become part of the ship itself. But Wyvern's next words gave Will hope.

"Open the chest with the key and stab the heart," old Wyvern cried, then seemed to suddenly change his mind. "Don't stab the heart! The *Dutchman* must have a living heart or there is no captain! And if there is no captain, there's no one to have the key!"

"The captain has the key?" Will asked, confused by Wyvern's ravings.

"Hidden," was all Wyvern said. He withdrew, once again becoming one with the hull of the ship.

But Will had his answer – and that was half of what he needed.

The key was with Jones.

Will headed for the deck.

Chapter 22

Aboard the *Black Pearl*, Jack Sparrow found Elizabeth filling in the names on the Letters of Marque that she'd taken from Lord Beckett.

Jack immediately snatched them away. "These Letters of Marque are supposed to go to *me*, are they not?"

Jack spotted the signature on the papers. "Lord Cutler Beckett. *He's* the man wants my Compass?"

Elizabeth hesitated. "Not the Compass, a chest."

The word caught Gibbs's attention. "A chest? Not the chest of Davy Jones? If the East India Trading Company controls the chest, they'll control the sea," Gibbs grumbled.

Elizabeth's ears perked up – control of the sea. So *that* was why Beckett was so eager to get his hands on the chest! It had nothing to do with Jack. She turned her attention back to the captain.

"Aye, a discomforting notion," the captain agreed. "May I inquire as to how you came by these?"

"Persuasion," Elizabeth answered.

Jack raised an eyebrow. "Friendly?" he asked with a smile.

"Decidedly not," Elizabeth snapped. She didn't have time for Jack's games – or his flirting.

Jack scowled and looked again at the letters. "Full pardon," he huffed. "Commission as a privateer on behalf of England and the East India Trading Company. As if I could be bought." He shook his head and stuffed the letters in his jacket pocket. "Not for this low of a price. Fate worse than death, living a life like that . . ."

"Jack," Elizabeth said. "The letters. Give them back."

Jack looked at her. "Persuade me," he said with a grin.

Elizabeth hesitated, then turned her back on the infuriating pirate who was smugly patting the Letters in his jacket pocket. Norrington had been standing nearby, listening in. As she passed by him to leave, he couldn't help but notice a small smile playing on her face.

"It's a curious thing," Norrington said, falling into step with Elizabeth. "There was a time when I'd have given anything for you to look like that while thinking of me. Just once."

Elizabeth stiffened at the suggestion that she might have an interest in Captain Jack. "I don't know what you mean," Elizabeth said.

"I think you do," Norrington insisted.

"Don't be absurd. I trust him, that's all."

"Ah," Norrington nodded. He turned to walk away, but not without one final thought to leave with Elizabeth.

"Did you never wonder how your fiancé ended up on the *Flying Dutchman* in the first place?" Norrington asked.

Chapter 23

Back on the *Dutchman*, Will had made his way to the main deck. A game of Liar's Dice was being played by a few of the crew.

Standing back a bit, Will observed the game and tried to follow along.

"I wager ten years!" Maccus said hotly.

Another crewman matched the ten years and the game was on. Each man bid a number, then Maccus peeked at the dice under his cup. "Four fives," he said firmly.

"Liar!" another crewman in the game called. Maccus cursed as he revealed his dice. The barnacled sea man had only three fives.

"What are they playing for?" Will asked Bootstrap, who had followed his son.

"The only thing any of us has," Bootstrap sighed, "years of service."

"Any member of the crew can be challenged?"

Will asked his father thoughtfully.

"Aye," Bootstrap replied.

"I challenge Davy Jones," Will boldly announced.

The crew went silent and, as if by magic, Jones appeared instantly on the deck. "Accepted," he told Will, eyeing him carefully. "But I only bet for what's dearest to a man's heart."

"I wager a hundred years of service," was Will's reply.

"No!" Bootstrap cried.

"Against your freedom?" Jones asked.

"My father's freedom." Will thought he had no need to wager against his own freedom. He thought he was already free, having no idea Jack had been bargaining with his soul.

"Agreed," Jones answered and took a seat across from Will. Jones eagerly rolled first. "You are a desperate man," Jones remarked. "You are the one who hopes to get married. But your fate is to be married to this ship."

"I choose my own fate," Will replied.

"Then it wouldn't be fate, would it?" Jones answered. "Five threes."

Will took a breath. "Five sixes," he said.

Jones looked in his eyes. "Liar."

Will revealed his dice. To the crew's shock, he had five sixes! "Well done, Master Turner," Jones said, rising to leave. Will had won the first round. His father was free.

But Will wasn't satisfied. "Another game," he said suddenly.

The crew gasped. "You can't best the devil twice, son," Jones said, cautioning him.

Will smiled knowingly. "Then why are you walking away?"

Jones's beard curled wildly. He didn't like to be goaded.

"The stakes?" Jones asked, taking his seat again.

"I wager my soul," Will answered. "An eternity of servitude."

"Against?" Jones asked.

"What was it you said about that which is dearest to a man's heart?" Will asked, presenting the cloth. "I want this."

Jones heaved his huge head. "How do you know of the key?" he snarled.

"That's not part of the game, is it?" Will asked.

Jones scowled as one of his tentacles

reached into his shirt and pulled out the key. It hung from a chain Jones wore around his neck. That's what Will needed to see. He now knew where the key was hidden, and he tried not to show his satisfaction. He slammed his cup down along with Jones's, when another cup suddenly slammed down, too.

"I'm in," Bootstrap said looking at Jones. "Matching his wager, an eternity in service to you." Not waiting for permission, Bootstrap began a new game. "I bid three twos," he said, looking at his dice under the cup.

"Don't do this," Will begged.

Too much was at stake now that his father was playing. If Will lost, he would join Jones's crew, but at least his father would be free. But if Bootstrap lost, he would again be bound to the ship, even though Will would go free.

"The die's been cast, Will. Your bid, Captain," Bootstrap said, ignoring his son's pleas.

Davy Jones checked his dice. "Four threes."

"Five threes," Will said reluctantly.

"Seven fives," Jones told them.

Will couldn't go any higher. "Eight fives," he said, bluffing.

Jones smiled. He knew Will was lying. "Welcome to the crew, lad."

"Twelve fives," Bootstrap yelled suddenly. Jones glowered at him, but Bootstrap held steady. "Call me a liar, or up the bid."

Jones slipped the key back into his shirt. "Bootstrap Bill, you are a liar, and you will spend an eternity of service to me on this ship. William Turner, feel free to go ashore . . . the very next time we make port." Jones laughed and moved off.

Will was furious. "You fool! Why did you do that?"

Bootstrap dropped his tired head and said, "I couldn't let you lose."

"It was never about winning or losing," Will said, sighing. Bootstrap stared at him for a moment, then suddenly understood . . . it was about finding the key. And Will had, at least, done that.

Chapter 24

Later that night, the merchant ship, the *Edinburgh Trader*, appeared on the horizon near the *Dutchman*. Grabbing Will, Bootstrap went to the railing and quietly pointed the *Trader* out to Will. "It's your chance," Bootstrap whispered.

Will nodded. But before he could get on the passing ship, he had something to take care of. He moved towards the captain's cabin and quietly slipped inside. Jones was asleep, sprawled across the organ. Will moved a step closer when Jones's finger suddenly hit a key. The noise echoed through the cabin, but the sleeping captain didn't move. Will held his breath and crept up to the organ. Pushing away Jones's tentacled beard, he reached for the key.

Just as Will had worked it off the chain, a single tentacle grabbed the key and tried to pull it back to Jones. Will looked down at the cloth that he still held in his hand. He rolled it up and quickly placed the cloth in the tentacle's grip. Satisfied to be holding something, the tentacle released the key and rested peacefully again with the cloth in its clutches.

Will retreated from the cabin and dashed back to Bootstrap. "Is she still there?" he asked, his eyes searching the dark sea for the *Trader*.

Bootstrap had readied a longboat for Will. "Aye, but the moment's slipping away."

Will's heart ached at leaving his father behind. He climbed over the side of the *Dutchman*. "Come with me," he pleaded.

"I can't. I'm part of the ship now, Will. I can't leave. Take this," he said, handing him a black knife from his belt. "Always meant for you to have it . . ."

Will smiled. "I will see you free of this prison. I promise you."

Will slipped into the longboat and disappeared on the dark waters of the night.

The next morning, a large crewman arrived to take Bootstrap's place on watch. He found the old pirate asleep and kicked him hard. "Show a leg, before the captain spots you."

Suddenly, the crewman's eyes fell on the white sails of the *Edinburgh Trader*. "All hands!" he bellowed. "Ship a quarter stern!"

Davy Jones came on deck and looked out to sea. "Who stood watch last night?"

The crew pushed Bootstrap forward. "How is it, Bootstrap, you let a ship pass by, unnoticed?" the tentacled captain asked.

"Beggin' your mercy, Capt'n, I fell sound asleep. Beggin' your mercy, it won't happen again."

"Bring the son," Jones ordered.

"He's not on board, sir," a crewman said. "One of the longboats is missing."

Jones immediately understood. He met Bootstrap's eye and watched the pirate's face grow pale. Jones pulled the chain from his shirt. The key was gone. There was only one person tricky enough to be behind this. "Jack Sparrow," he shouted. "Captain Jack Sparrow!"

Chapter 25

In the captain's cabin of the *Edinburgh Trader*, Will huddled underneath a blanket and clutched a warm drink in his hand. As he began to thaw out, Captain Bellamy tried to understand what was going on. "Strange thing, to come upon a longboat so far out in open waters," he said.

"Just put as many leagues behind us as you can, as fast as you can," Will replied. His eyes fell on Elizabeth's wedding dress, thrown casually across a chair.

"That dress. Where did you get it?" Will asked.

"Funny, that dress," Captain Bellamy said. "Found aboard the ship. Put quite a stir into the crew, thought it was a spirit, bringing an omen of ill fate. But it brought good fortune! The spirit told us, put in at Tortuga, and we made a nice bit of profit there – off the books."

Will ran his fingers over the white fabric and smiled. "I imagine some of your crew might have jumped ship there?"

"Bound to happen," Bellamy said with a wave of his hand.

A sailor on deck suddenly rushed to the cabin. "Captain! A ship's been spotted!"

"Colours?" Bellamy asked.

"She's not flying any, sir," the sailor replied.

"Pirates," Bellamy said, glancing warily at Will.

"Or worse," Will cried, rushing out on to the deck. He climbed the yard arm and looked out at the water.

"It's the *Dutchman!*" Will cried. "I've doomed us all."

Will had barely finished speaking when the *Edinburgh Trader* lurched to a sudden stop. "Mother Cary's chickens!" the bursar shouted in alarm. "What happened?"

"Must have hit a reef," the quartermaster answered. After all, large ships did not just stop of their own accord.

Captain Bellamy looked over the rail, trying to see what had halted them. The sea looked empty. "Free the rudder!" he commanded. "Hard to port, then starboard and back again!"

The sailors followed orders and turned for more instructions. But Bellamy was gone. The crew looked out toward the sea, where what appeared to be a tiny figure was wrapped in a huge tentacle. As the crew looked closer, it was clear to them that the figure was the captain! The tentacle rose high in the air and then slapped the screaming captain down upon the water.

"KRAKEN!" the crew shouted in terror.

Having taken out the captain, the Kraken came back for the ship. The arms of the huge creature swept over the deck and smashed the longboats.

In a spray of wood and sea foam, the Kraken broke the ship in two and pulled it under.

When it was over, six men kneeled on the deck of the *Flying Dutchman*. "Where is the son?" Jones asked, studying the line of terrified sailors. "And where is the key?"

"No sign," Maccus answered. "He must have been claimed by the sea."

"I *am* the sea!" Jones bellowed angrily.

"Overboard!" he shouted, motioning to the doomed sailors. They were of no use to him.

As his crewman tossed the last survivors of the merchant ship over the side, Jones paced the deck. "The chest is no longer safe," he growled, knowing that Bootstrap's son had the key. He also knew Will was working with Jack. "Crowd on sail and gather way. Chart a course to *Isla Cruces*."

"He won't find the chest," a crewman said.

"He knew about the key, didn't he?" Jones shouted impatiently. He would not risk Jack discovering the location of his heart. He needed to get to *Isla Cruces* before Will – or Jack – arrived. "Get me there first," Jones shouted. "Or there be the devil to pay!"

Holding fast to the stern of the *Dutchman* and able to hear every word on deck, the sole survivor of the *Edinburgh Trader*, Will Turner, now knew where the chest was hidden. Crouching down on the stern, he was suddenly filled with hope. He had a ride to the chest . . . and the key in his pocket!

Chapter 26

While Will was hitching a ride to *Isla Cruces* on the *Dutchman*, Jack was heading for the same island on the *Black Pearl*. Jack's Compass, in Elizabeth's hand, had finally given him proper direction.

But Elizabeth didn't seem very happy.

"Elizabeth, are you well? Everything shipshape and Bristol fashion? My tremendous intuitive sense of the female creature informs me you are troubled," Jack gallantly said.

Elizabeth let out a sigh. "I just thought I'd be married by now," she said.

Jack smiled agreeably. "I like marriage! It's like a wager on who will fall out of love first."

Elizabeth moved away, but Jack pursued her. "You know, I am captain of a ship. I could perform a marriage right here on this deck, right now."

"No, thank you," Elizabeth said to his hasty proposal.

"Why not?" he asked her, smiling. "Admit it, we are so much alike, you and I. I and you."

"Except for a, oh, a sense of decency and honour," Elizabeth said. "And a moral centre. And personal hygiene."

Jack looked himself over. "Trifles!" he said quickly. "You will come over to my side, in time. I know."

"You seem quite certain."

Jack nodded. "One word, love. Curiosity. You long for freedom. To do what you want because you want it. To act on selfish impulse. You want to see what it's like. Someday," he said, looking into her eyes, "you won't be able to resist."

Elizabeth's expression was stonelike. With a chill in her voice, she replied, "Because you and I are alike, there will come a moment when you have the chance to show it – to do the right thing."

Jack brightened. "I love those moments! I like to wave as they pass by!"

Elizabeth ignored him. "You will have a chance to do something brave," she told him. "And in that moment you will discover something."

Jack looked at her as if he couldn't imagine

what on earth that something might be. He looked puzzled, as if he were trying to figure it out.

"That you are a good man!" Elizabeth told him, finally.

"All evidence to the contrary," Jack pointed out.

"I have faith in you. Do you know why? Curiosity," she said confidently. "You're going to want it. A chance to be admired and gain the rewards that follow. You won't be able to resist."

Jack opened his mouth to retort but was stopped by a loud command, "Land, ho!"

Jack raced to the rail. He could see the tiny island of *Isla Cruces* on the horizon. He stared down into the suddenly still water. The island was too far away for Jack's taste. "I want my jar," he said meekly.

Chapter 27

Captain Jack Sparrow sat in a longboat, clutching his jar of dirt like a frightened child. Opposite him were Elizabeth and Norrington, both trying to take seriously what they saw as the captain's ridiculous behaviour. Pintel and Ragetti were rowing the longboat toward *Isla Cruces*.

"You're pulling too fast," Pintel complained to his one-eyed friend.

"You're pulling too slow," Ragetti answered. "We don't want the Kraken to catch us."

Jack cringed at the mention of the sea monster's name.

"I'm saving me strength for when it comes," Pintel said. "And I don't think it's 'Krack-en', anyways. I always heard it said 'Kray-ken'."

Jack cringed again. "What, with a long *a*? 'Krock-en' is how it is in the original

Scandinavian," Ragetti answered, leaning on the oars. "And 'Krack-en' is closer to that."

They heard a sudden splash in the water and the two took to rowing faster. They could debate later.

Reaching the shore, Jack gratefully hopped out. He took off his jacket, patted the pocket to make sure the Letters of Marque were still there, placed them and the jar in the longboat's bow and grabbed a shovel. "Guard the boat. Mind the tide," he ordered Pintel and Ragetti. Jack thrust the Compass into Elizabeth's hands and they made their way up the beach.

"I didn't expect anyone to be here," Norrington said, when they came upon an abandoned church.

"There's not," Elizabeth answered.

"You know this place?" he asked, surprised.

"Stories," Elizabeth said, moving on. "The Church came to the island and brought salvation, and disease and death. They say the priest had to bury everybody, one after the other. It drove him mad and he hung himself."

"Better mad with the rest of the world than sane alone," Norrington noted. Elizabeth stared at him. Norrington had changed so much since she first met him. This cynical man was not the commodore she had once known.

"No fraternizing with the help, love," Jack said, interrupting her thoughts. Elizabeth scowled, looked down at the Compass and continued to walk. Suddenly, the needle began to swing wildly – they had found the spot! Jack drew an X in the sand with the toe of his boot and handed the shovel to Norrington.

At the same time, on an outer reef of *Isla Cruces*, the *Flying Dutchman* came around the point. Through his spyglass, Davy Jones saw the longboat. "They're here," he scowled, stomping the deck. "And I cannot step foot on land again for near of a decade!"

"Ye'll trust us to act in yer stead?" Maccus asked him.

"I trust you to know what awaits should you fail!" Jones promised. "Down, then," he ordered his crew.

Maccus nodded and called out, "Down, down." The bow of the *Flying Dutchman* submerged into the blue sea, bubbles rushing over her deck. In a moment, the entire ship went under and moved beneath the waves as swiftly as if it were being pushed down by a huge, invisible hand. Fish darted by as the *Dutchman* headed, beneath the waves, for *Isla Cruces*, churning the sea above her to foam.

Sitting on the beach, Pintel and Ragetti stared out at the boiling sea and turned to each other in terror. Springing to their feet, they left the longboat and ran to warn the others.

Chapter 28

Time was running out for Jack. He and Elizabeth stood anxiously over the hole Norrington had dug. They gave a start when the shovel suddenly clanked against something hard. They had hit the chest! Jack jumped into the hole and helped lift it out.

Jack quickly broke the lock with the shovel. He sank to his knees and opened the chest. Inside were the mementoes of a love lost; a strand of white pearls and a long white dress, dried flowers and faded love letters. Jack pushed the stuff aside and found a box. He lifted the box from the chest. It was bound in bands of iron and locked tightly, but the sound of a single deep beat could be heard coming from inside.

"It's real!" Elizabeth gasped.

Norrington was astounded. "You actually were telling the truth."

Jack raised an eyebrow. "I do that a lot, and yet people are still surprised."

"With good reason," came a voice.

The group turned to see Will Turner. He approached them, out of breath and soaked to the skin.

With a gasp of astonishment, Elizabeth rushed to him. "Will – you're all right!" She threw her arms around his neck.

Jack looked behind Will, worriedly. "How did you get here?" he asked.

"Sea turtles, mate. A pair of them, strapped to my feet," Will said, referencing a well-known legend that Jack Sparrow himself had escaped an island on the backs of turtles.

Jack grinned at Will's slight. "Not so easy, is it?"

"But I do owe you thanks, Jack," Will said. "After you tricked me onto that ship to square your debt to Jones—"

"What?" Elizabeth said, looking at Jack.

"—I was reunited with my father."

Jack gulped. "You're welcome."

"Everything you said to me – *every word* was a lie?" Elizabeth said, glaring at Jack.

"Yes. Time and tide, love," Jack nodded with no apology. Then the cocky expression left his face as he noticed Will kneeling beside the chest. Will had the key in one hand, the knife his father had given him in the other.

"What are you doing?" Jack asked.

"I'm going to kill Jones," Will answered.

In a flash, a cool blade was pressed against Will's throat. It was Jack's blade.

"I can't let you do that, William," Jack said. "If Jones is dead, then who's to call his beastie off the hunt? Now, if you please – the key."

Quick as lightning, Will slapped Jack's sword away, jumped back and grabbed the cutlass Elizabeth had been carrying since her trip to Tortuga. "I keep the promises I make," he said, facing off with Jack. "I intend to free my father."

But suddenly, Norrington drew his sword and turned it on Will. "I can't let you do that, either. Sorry."

Jack looked at the former commodore and grinned. "I knew you'd warm up to me eventually," he said, delighted with the sudden turn of events.

Norrington pointed his sword quickly toward Jack, and revealed his true intention. "Lord Beckett desires the contents of that chest. If I deliver it, I get my life back."

"Ah, the dark side of ambition," Jack sighed grimly.

The three men instantly sprung forward, their swords locked together in a clash of steel.

"Will," Jack said urgently, "we can't let him get the chest. You can trust me on this!" Will held his sword steady, his eyes wide with disbelief. "You can mistrust me less than you can mistrust him," Jack finally offered.

Will stopped to consider, then looked at Norrington. "You look awful," he said to the bedraggled commodore.

"Granted," Norrington replied. "But you're still naïve. Jack just wants Elizabeth for himself."

"Pot. Kettle. Black," Jack said, summing up the situation in three words.

The three men sprung back, clashing swords again.

"Guard the chest," Will told Elizabeth as he, Norrington and Jack swung wildly at each other.

"No! This is barbaric! This is not how grown men settle their affairs!" Elizabeth shouted. They paid her no attention.

From between the palms, Ragetti, who had made it safely off the beach, had been watching the scene. "Now, how'd this a-go all screwy?" Pintel asked, arriving beside him and crouching low. They both eyed the chest.

Ragetti sighed. "Each wants the chest for hisself. Mr Norrington, I think, is hopin' to regain a bit of honour, ol' Jack's looking to trade it to save his own skin and Turner there . . . he's tryin' to settle some unresolved business 'twixt him and his twice-cursed pirate father."

"Sad," Pintel commented. "That chest must be worth more'n a shiny penny. If we was any kind of decent, we'd remove temptation from their path." The two pirates gave each other a sideways glance and crept towards the chest.

Elizabeth was still trying to stop the wild sword fight, but nothing seemed to help. She fell to the sand, pretending to faint in the hope that the men would halt their battle and help her. She lay still as long as she could, then opened her eyes in time to catch Pintel and Ragetti making off into the jungle with the chest.

Jumping to her feet, she was torn for a moment between telling Will or chasing the chest. She narrowed her eyes as she saw the three men slashing away at each other in the distance, and decided to duck into the jungle and go after the pirates.

Chapter 29

The fight was in full swing and moving all over the island.

Norrington shoved Will back hard and the key was dropped.

"Hah-hah!" Jack howled, watching the key fly into the air before landing squarely in his hand. Norrington and Will stood stunned as Jack took off down the beach with the key, then quickly regained their composure and bolted after him.

Jack headed for the old church. Racing into the bell tower, key in hand, he climbed the wooden stairs. High above him, dangling from the timbers, was the skeleton of the legendary hanged priest. Jack gave the skeleton a quick nod and continued his climb.

Norrington and Will quickly caught up with Jack on the stairs. Norrington started swinging his sword at Jack. But Jack stepped aside just in time. The weapon whistled as it moved past his arm. With a grunt, Norrington slammed Jack with the hilt of his sword, grabbed the key and flung Jack from the stairway.

As Jack fell, he reached out and grabbed the bell-tower rope that held the priest's skeleton. Jack and the skeleton both dropped straight down. Will grabbed the second rope and was hoisted up just as Jack was making his way down. Will snatched the key from Norrington as he passed him near the top of the tower. When Will reached the top of the tower, the church bell began to toll.

Chapter 30

Down on the beach, a gentle ripple appeared in the water. Slowly and eerily, the heads of Jones's crew rose from the pale blue water and the fearsome gang stalked ashore. They gathered at the now-empty, recently dug hole.

Suddenly, the sound of the church bells drew the crew's attention to the tower. They watched as Will Turner stepped out onto the church's rooftop.

Will was trying to get away – from Jack, from Norrington and now from Jones's crew. He jumped across a break in the roof as Norrington slashed at him over the gaping void. Using the point of his sword, Norrington nimbly lifted the key from Will's grasp. The former commodore felt the sudden weight of the key as it dropped into his hand, then felt it disappear just as quickly as Jack snatched it away from him.

Norrington turned in a rage and knocked Jack's sword from his hand. He looked over his shoulder at Will. "Excuse me while I kill the man who ruined my life," he said, pardoning himself.

"Be my guest," Will answered, finally relaxing for a moment.

Jack raised a finger. "Let's examine that claim for a moment, shall we, former commodore?"

Will couldn't help but smile as Jack once again tried to turn the odds in his favour. "Who was the man who, at the moment you had a notorious pirate safely behind bars and a beautiful dolly belle bound for the bridal, saw fit to free said pirate and take your dearly beloved for himself?" Jack nodded toward Will.

Norrington didn't let Jack continue. "Enough!" he roared, slashing wildly at Jack. Unarmed, Jack threw up his hands and slid down the roof screaming. The key dropped to the ground.

"Good show!" Will said, clapping.

"Unfortunately, Mr Turner," Norrington said, turning his blade on Will, "he's right." Norrington hated Jack, but he wasn't fond of Will, either.

Below them, Jack took advantage of the

fight above, grabbing the key and running. "Still rooting for you, mate!" he called up to Will as swords clashed.

Jack slowed to a walk and put the key over his neck. Just when he thought he was safe, he stumbled into an open grave.

As Jack tried to get out of the hole, Will leapt onto a mill wheel that was attached to the side of the church. The old wheel creaked under his weight. Norrington jumped on as well and, with a huge crash, the wheel suddenly broke free. Will and Norrington steadied their legs to keep balanced.

Just as Jack finally pulled himself out from the grave, he was caught up by the rolling wheel. The key fell away from Jack's neck and was hooked on a splintered nail on the surface of the wheel. A moment later Jack was thrown off the wheel. He had lost the key – again! He sighed and then took off after the runaway wheel.

Chapter 31

Meanwhile, in the small island's jungle, Elizabeth had finally caught up with Pintel and Ragetti.

"'Ello, poppet," Pintel said, grinning, as Elizabeth confronted them. He and Ragetti set down the chest and drew their swords. Elizabeth reached for hers but suddenly remembered Will had taken it. Slowly, she began to back away.

The two pirates were about to attack when something came crashing through the jungle. The three turned to see the mill wheel roll past with Jack running at full speed behind it.

Pintel and Ragetti shrugged, focusing again on Elizabeth. Suddenly, a barnacle-encrusted axe hit a tree next to Ragetti's head with a twang. Jones's crew had arrived.

Pintel and Ragetti dropped their swords at Elizabeth's feet in horror. They grabbed the chest and made a run for it. Elizabeth took a sword in each hand, racing through the trees behind them.

Running as fast as they could, and still holding the chest, the pirates tried to pass on either side of a tree and slammed the chest smack into its trunk. Jones's crew suddenly burst through the jungle. Looking at the trunk, then at the imposing and terrifying crew, Ragetti, Pintel and Elizabeth made a quick decision: the three of them took off at lightning speed and left the chest behind.

On another part of the island, a chase was still going on. Jack was after the wheel, which held the key to what was *in* the chest. He picked up some speed and, for the first time, was running *next* to the wheel instead of *behind* it. Focusing on the key as it looped around, Jack timed his move perfectly and jumped back into the wheel.

From his spot on top, Will saw what Jack was doing. Will reached down, grabbed the key from the nail and swung himself back inside the wheel. Norrington was quick to follow. Slashing at Will, Jack grabbed the key, climbed up to the top and then jumped into a nearby palm tree.

Dangling from the palm, Jack noticed one of Jones's crew members coming – and he was carrying the chest! Jack reached for a coconut. Happy with the weight of it, he hurled it at the crewman's head.

Jack saw the undead crewman's head roll off as it was thwacked by his well-aimed coconut. He jumped down. No other crewmen were in sight. With the key in his hand and almost unable to believe his good fortune, he carefully approached the chest.

Jack took a breath. Kneeling beside the chest, he turned the key in the lock. His eyes widened as he finally saw what he'd been searching for: Jones's heart. Taking off his shirt, he reached into the chest and wrapped the heart safely up. Then he glanced around one more time, to make sure he hadn't been spotted, and took off.

Jack dashed directly to the longboat. He reached into the bow and grabbed his jar. Emptying some of the dirt onto the beach, he placed the covered heart inside and filled the jar back up with sand.

Jack looked up when he heard a sudden commotion. Bursting from the jungle came

Pintel, Ragetti and Elizabeth. They were once again hauling the chest and Jones's crewman were close behind them.

Elizabeth bravely slashed away at Jones's crew, but her efforts were increasingly futile. She was about to be overrun when the huge wheel came crashing out of the jungle.

The wheel rolled over several of Jones's crewmen, which allowed Elizabeth to catch up to Pintel and Ragetti as they dragged the chest through the sand towards the longboat.

Jack gritted his teeth, unhappy with how crowded the beach had become. He tucked his jar back into the bow and raised an oar, ready to shove off or fight.

The huge wheel finally lumbered to the waterline and tilted over with a splash. Will and Norrington dizzily climbed out. Norrington staggered over to the longboat and collapsed over the edge. He lifted his head and his eyes fell on Jack's jar. He reached into the bow.

Jack held his breath. He watched as Norrington's hand moved past the jar and reached for the Letters of Marque in his coat pocket. Jack didn't try to stop him. He had no need for those papers now, not when he had the heart that controlled Davy Jones and safe passage or peril for every ship that sailed the seven seas.

As Jack contemplated his good fortune, the fight on the beach raged on. It was now Sparrow's crew versus Jones's crew – and Jones seemed to have the advantage.

Suddenly, through the chaos, Will noticed the chest. The key was still in the lock. He leaned down to open it as Jack quickly spun around with an oar in his hand and whacked him in the head. Will dropped to the beach, unconscious. Rushing to his side, Elizabeth looked down at her fiancé.

"We're not getting out of this," Elizabeth said to Norrington, when she realized just how desperate the situation had become.

"Not with the chest," he replied, knowing what had to happen. He grabbed the chest and ordered her into the boat. "Don't wait for me," he called back and disappeared from the beach into the jungle. Jones's crew took off after him.

"I say we respect his final wish," Jack said quickly from his spot nearby.

"Aye!" Pintel agreed and began pushing the longboat into the surf. Jack hopped in and grabbed his jar. He had the heart, but didn't want to take any chances. Holding on to the heart, and Tia Dalma's dirt inside the jar, he'd be safe.

"We have to take Will," Elizabeth ordered. Jack rolled his eyes but nodded his head, and Pintel and Ragetti hauled Will into the longboat. Without another word, they pushed off . . . leaving Norrington behind.

Chapter 32

Moments later, Jack's crew, minus Norrington, was back on the main deck of the *Black Pearl*. Will slowly opened his eyes. "What happened to the chest?" he asked groggily.

"Norrington took it – to draw them off," Elizabeth answered.

Gibbs appeared on deck and welcomed them all back. He was ready to make sail. "Jack!" he said. "We spied the *Dutchman* an hour past, rounding the point!"

"Is that so?" Jack replied with a confident look in his eye.

Gibbs gave his captain a funny look. He didn't have time to try to work out what was going on. There was a dangerous ship – the *most* dangerous ship to ever sail the seas – far too close. "All hands! Set sail! Run her full!" Gibbs shouted.

As the *Pearl*'s crew scrambled to get under-way, Jack felt no need to rush. He sat down on a barrel, his legs dangling, and cradled his precious jar.

"Gibbs, is your throat tight?" he asked.

"Aye," Gibbs answered.

Jack nodded. "Your heart beats fast, your breath is short, you have an acute awareness of the vulnerability of your own skin?"

"Aye! Aye!"

"I fear you suffer from the malady of intense and overwhelming fear," Jack observed casually.

"What's into you? We've got only half a chance at best – and that's if the wind holds!" Gibbs said, not understanding Jack's attitude. Only a few hours before, Jack had been a bundle of nerves himself.

Elizabeth walked to the rail. For once, she had to agree with Jack. "We are in no danger," she said to Gibbs. "I see empty horizon in all directions."

She had spoken too soon. As they watched in horror, the ocean began to bubble and foam. Suddenly, with a mighty splash, the *Flying Dutchman* shot up from below the sea. It settled down right next to the *Pearl*, sending a wave over her decks.

"Hard to port! Steal his wind! Full canvas!" Gibbs shouted with all his might.

As the crew worked furiously at their stations, Jack turned toward the *Dutchman*. Lifting the jar over his head, he pointed to it, nodded, smiled and gave a friendly wave.

At the helm of the *Flying Dutchman*, Davy Jones pulled back as if he'd been struck, realizing that Jack must have his heart.

"Ready the cannons," Jones said to Maccus.

Jack yelled out to the *Dutchman*, "Over here! Yoo-hoo! Parlay!"

Gibbs moved alongside. "What's your play, Jack?"

"Shhh!" Jack replied. He thumped the jar. "I have the heart. In here," Jack whispered.

"Bless me! How?" Gibbs asked.

Jack smiled. "I'm Captain Jack Sparrow, remember?"

Gibbs sighed as he watched the cannon ports on the *Dutchman* opening. Jack thought he was invincible, but Gibbs knew better – he had to protect the ship. "Hard a' port!" he shouted, turning his attention back to the ship. "Hurry, men!"

Jack's crew scrambled and the *Black Pearl* tacked hard, leaving the *Dutchman* at her stern.

A blast of cannon fire suddenly came from the *Dutchman's* forward guns. "Into the swells! Go square to the wind! Come on!" Gibbs yelled, adjusting course.

The *Dutchman* fired again, but the *Pearl* was pulling away. "She's falling behind!" Elizabeth cheered.

"Aye! With the wind, we've got her!" Gibbs nodded proudly.

"The *Black Pearl* can outrun the *Dutchman*?" Will asked him.

"That ain't a natural ship," Gibbs said, nodding at the *Flying Dutchman*. "It can sail direct against the wind, into a hurricane and not lose speed. That's how she takes her prey. But with the wind . . ."

"We rob her advantage," Will said, suddenly understanding.

"Aye," Gibbs said. "The *Pearl* is the only ship Davy Jones fears. With reason."

Chapter 33

Jack smiled as the *Pearl* sped farther and farther away from the *Dutchman*. He held his jar close.

"If we can outrun her, we can take her!" Will said, rushing to Jack on deck. "We should turn and fight!"

"Or flee like the cowardly weasels we are," Jack answered brightly.

"You've the only ship as can match the *Dutchman*! In a fair fight we've got half a chance."

"That's not much incentive for me to fight fair, is it?" Jack answered, drumming upon his jar.

Suddenly, the *Black Pearl* lurched. Sailors tumbled forwards. Jack's jar was knocked free from his hands and shattered, sending sand and dirt all over the deck. He dropped to his knees and pawed through it. There was nothing more than the dirt and sand.

Jack looked up at Gibbs and swallowed hard. "Um. I *don't* have the heart."

"Then who does?" Gibbs asked, as the *Pearl* groaned and shuddered to a stop. Jack went pale. He had neither Jones's heart nor Tia Dalma's dirt.

Elizabeth looked out over the rail as the *Pearl* ground to a halt.

"We must have hit a reef!" she called out.

Will frowned, he'd heard those same words aboard the *Edinburgh Trader*. "No! It's not a reef! Get away from the rail!"

"What is it?" Elizabeth asked, seeing the terror in Will's eyes.

"The Kraken," was all Gibbs said.

Chapter 34

The deck of the *Pearl* grew silent as Gibbs's words sunk in. The Kraken had finally found Jack.

On the floor of the ship, Jack had stopped sifting through the dirt and sand. It was no use. The heart was not there and the Black Spot had reappeared on his hand. He was marked, the situation was hopeless – he was doomed.

As quietly as possible, Jack headed towards the *Pearl*'s stern. None of the crew members noticed as he slipped into a longboat and rowed away from his ship.

The water around the *Pearl* began to churn and bubble, indicating the arrival of the Kraken. Then the terrible creature appeared from the depths, tentacles held high above the crew.

"To arms!" Will shouted. "Defend the masts! Don't let it get a grip." The pirates ran to their stations and prepared for the coming attack. Cannons were loaded and masts made ready.

Slowly, the Kraken's tentacles made their way over the railings. But Will had known that the Kraken would attack on the starboard side from his earlier encounter with the creature, and the cannons were ready. With a powerful command from Will, the cannons were fired. The Kraken was blown away – its body twisting in pain as it sank back away from the ship, smashing the longboats as it went down.

"It will be back!" Will yelled. Turning to Elizabeth he added, "Get off the ship."

"No boats," Elizabeth replied. The Kraken had destroyed every last one of them. Or *almost* every last one . . .

As the Kraken was getting ready to attack again, Jack was working on getting away in his longboat as quickly as possible. But there was something stopping him from making a clean break. He looked down at his Compass and watched the needle swing to its mark – the *Black Pearl* and his crew.

With a sigh, Jack began to row.

* * *

Back on the *Pearl*, it looked as if the Kraken was going to win this battle. Nothing the pirates did to stop the monster worked. They shot at it, stabbed at it, threw nets at it – but the beast kept coming.

Elizabeth stood in the captain's cabin, a rifle in her shaking hands. She knew Jack had disappeared and was furious. How could he leave at a time like this? He was the one the Kraken was looking for. He had got them into this mess. Then tentacles slowly moved through the windows and started towards her.

Stumbling, she dropped the rifle, headed towards the deck and ran straight into Jack. He was back.

"We've got some time. Abandon ship!" he ordered, ignoring Elizabeth's look of surprise.

"What chance do we have in a boat?" Will asked, coming over to Jack.

"Very little. But we can make for the island. We can get away as it takes down the *Pearl*!" As Jack said this, his eyes grew sad. There was no choice. The Kraken would return and the *Pearl* would go under. They had to get away.

Following orders, Will, Gibbs and the rest

of the crew headed toward the longboat. But Elizabeth lingered behind.

"Thank you, Jack," Elizabeth said softly. Moving closer towards him, she added, "You came back. I always knew you were a good man."

Leaning forward, Elizabeth kissed the pirate, then stepped back slowly.

CLICK.

Jack glanced down. Elizabeth had chained him to the mast of the boat while they kissed. "It's after you, not the ship – not us. It's the only way," she explained.

"Pirate," Jack said, with admiration.

Elizabeth took one last look at the pirate who had been the cause of so much trouble in her life and the cause of so much adventure. She rushed off the ship and left Jack . . . waiting.

Slowly, the tentacles of the Kraken snaked on board. With a mighty roar, the creature rose up in front of him, its mouth gaping and its breath deadly. And there before Jack, in the teeth of the mighty Kraken, was his lost, beloved hat. He plucked it out of the monster's mouth and placed it back on his head where it belonged.

"Hello, beastie," Jack said.

From the longboat, the crew of the *Black Pearl* watched as the Kraken and Jack battled. Slowly, the entire ship was covered by the terrible creature. With one mighty splash the ship, and Jack with it, was taken below the waves.

On board the *Flying Dutchman*, Davy Jones smiled. "Jack Sparrow," he said with satisfaction, "our debt is settled."

But Jones was not the only soul watching from the *Dutchman*. Bootstrap Bill was looking on as well. As Jack went down with the ship, Bootstrap's eyes grew wide with shock. What was left of his cursed heart wrenched.

With eyes full of sorrow, Bootstrap Bill looked out towards the still water where Jack and the *Pearl* had so recently been sailing. He remembered Jack Sparrow – *Captain* Jack Sparrow – with a heavy heart. Quietly and painfully, Bill whispered to the empty sea, "If any man could beat the devil, I'd have thought it would be you."

The *Black Pearl* was gone, along with her captain. And, already, the world seemed a bit less bright without them.